The Wickett Sisters in Hell

Ob la di, Ob la da, Life goes on, bra,
La la, How the life goes on.
Ob la di, Ob la da, Life goes on, bra,
La la, How the life goes on.

—Lennon and McCartney
 The White Album

*For Butch, One of a Kind Friend
(and thanks, Clara!)*

Copyright © 2017 by Stephen Houser

Lionel A. Blanchard, Publisher

All rights reserved. No part of this publication may be reproduced, stored in a retrieval system, or transmitted, in any form or by any means, electronic, mechanical, photocopying, recording, or otherwise, without the prior written permission of the author.

This is a work of fiction. Names, characters, places, and incidents either are the product of the author's imagination or are used fictitiously. Any resemblance to actual persons, living or dead, events, or locales is entirely coincidental.

First Printing

Cover Art and Design by Vincent Chong

Printed in the United States of America

The Wickett Sisters in Hell

A Novel by Stephen Houser

Chapter One

Mardie Wickett took baby steps across her kitchen floor. The painted tiles from Seville were slick as ice. One careless slip and who knew what would break, and broken didn't heal up real well down here. Stayed troublesome and painful. As long as you lasted.

One step, two. Three step, four. Good thing I'm a patient old broad, she thought, counting each mincing step. She paused to take a glance at herself in the wall mirror. Dyed blond hair down to her shoulders. Face still pretty, big blue eyes and nice cheekbones, just older than most men would look at twice. She primped her hair a little and stood up straight. She was still slim, with D-cup breasts holding their own and a rump that hadn't gone completely south. If she put a bag over her head she could pass for sixty. Maybe sixty-two. Either way it wasn't bad for sixty-eight. The trouble was she felt both the six and the eight in her joints and her back and everywhere else her bones still moved.

Mardie stretched out her hand and grasped a corner of the stove, a cast iron Andre Godin from France. It was done in black enamel with copper knobs, had a brass-plated door, and gold and silver curlicues painted in its nooks and crannies. Her body had once been like that, little pleasure spots hiding in every bend and cleft. Those were the days. And nights. Sad to say, her libido was mostly gone now. But then so were her lovers. Only one remained to strum her last filament of desire and she hadn't seen him for weeks.

Mardie picked up the teakettle and filled it at the sink. She sniffed the water through the spout. Didn't smell dangerous today. She opened the stove door and poked the embers. A small array of flames sprang up. She added a handful of kindling and placed the kettle on the stove. All in all it was a bit of a process to make morning tea, but as she had nothing better to do, and was a Brit, it endured as a pleasant ritual.

She carefully leaned her hip against a kitchen counter and waited for the water to boil. She'd read that doctors were still trying to figure out if elderly people broke their hips falling on the floor, or whether their hips broke first and then plunged them to their fate. Who cares, Mardie thought. Either way you wound up limping the rest of your life.

She filled her teacup with hot water, tossed in a pinch of tea, then set the cup and saucer on the table, its marquetry surface protected by a slab of glass. The colored woods had been inlaid with a mathematical precision worthy of M. C. Escher. In fact, Mauk himself had stopped by to see it once, and had liked it very much. The dealer who'd sold her the table had been charmingly insistent that it had been manufactured by the same Berlin workshop that had produced the gorgeous marquetry doors for King Philip of Spain's *la comunidad del Real Monasteriel del San Lorenzo de El Escorial*. Mardie found the dazzling doors a surprisingly joyful acquisition for a man who had spent his entire life thinking about death and worrying about damnation. He was obsessed by Hieronymus Bosch's canvases of Hell, and disbursed agents all across the continent to buy them.

Chapter One

He would stare at them for hours, mesmerized by the whippings, roastings, flayings, fryings, and beheadings visited upon those who had fallen short of God's grace. Frantically banking his own merits, he cleansed Spain of Jews and Muslims, burned Lutherans all over Europe, and found meaningful labor for ten million black and Indian slaves mining his silver in the new world. Alas, despite these and other pious efforts, Philip's paintings wound up in the Prado, and he wound up down here.

Mardie sipped her tea and surveyed her kitchen. She loved it, and she loved to cook in it. There were maple cupboards, stained dark and rich, a butcher-block island that she circled like a bouncing Maasai when she chopped, Dutch blue-and-white tile counter backsplashes with scenes of children skating on frozen canals, cheerful lace curtains with embroidered daisies and tulips on her one narrow window, an antique wooden ice box, which was altogether more reliable than any refrigerator she'd ever had, and, of course, her beloved stove.

The phone rang, a skinny black upright with a hook and a receiver. It rang and rang. Mardie stared at it. Who could be calling this early in the morning? She finally reached over and picked up.

"Yes?"

"Is this Mardell Wickett?" a formal baritone voice asked, its timbre abraded by too many cigarettes. No image appeared on the monitor connected to the phone. Mardie shrugged. It failed as often as her neighbor's bladder.

"No," she replied. "This is Mardie *or* Ms. Wickett, but definitely not Mardell."

There was a pause.

"Ms. Wickett, Lord Lucifer requires your presence at his headquarters this afternoon."

Mardie frowned. This place was the land of tricks, but this was a new one.

"Who is this?" she asked, suspicious now.

There was another pause.

"Who I am is of no consequence," the caller finally responded, his tone noticeably stiffer.

"I'm sure that's true enough," Mardie said, each word flicking off her tongue with disdain, "but I still want to know your name."

"All you need to know," the caller replied, ignoring Mardie's sarcastic remark, "is that the Master wants to see you this afternoon. Do you think you could manage to confirm that you understand and will comply?"

Mardie frowned. Righteous indignation from a scammer?

"Don't talk down to me," she hissed into the receiver. "Devil doesn't see anybody."

"Satan sees who he wants to see, Ms. Wickett," the voice countered instantly, rumbling ominously.

"Is that so? Well, I can't imagine why he would want to see me."

"You don't have to imagine," the caller replied, struggling with his temper. "He'll explain it face-to-face."

"Well, I'm not in the mood to wait. I'm not taking a single step out of my house unless you explain it right now."

There was another pause.

"There's been a murder," the speaker replied, quietly. "In Hell."

That was impossible. Mardie shook her head, annoyed.

"Fella, you overplayed your hand," she scoffed. "A murder in Hell? Why don't you call me back when you have a better line to pitch? Actually, why don't you just not call me back at all?"

Chapter One

Mardie hung the phone receiver on its hook, humiliated at being taken for grossly stupid by the anonymous caller. The anonymous *demon*. Satan's legions ran everything down here, and they were nasty, condescending assholes. She wondered for the umpteenth time what kind of total jerk Satan must be to have put them in charge.

Mardie picked up her teacup and took a sip. *A murder in Hell.* She frowned. As if. Lucifer was ageless and immortal and so, apparently, were his hordes of devils, demons, imps, and sprites. Some spirits from his countless cache of ne'er-do-wells had been assigned specific roles by their master, but many appeared to roam footloose and unsupervised, and the more freedom they had, the more actively hostile they were toward Hell's captive souls.

She had no idea how many kinds of demons there were, but everyone knew about the worst ones. There were Migards, nuisance devils shaped like snakes that snuggled up to the unwary in their beds and sucked up their body heat, and the shadowlike Draculs who took more from sleepers than their warmth. Mardie always checked her neck in the mirror in the morning. No fang marks so far. Unfortunately, no hickies either.

Everyone had seen Bast pleasure demons, dark-skinned, bare-chested females with the heads of cats. They frequented sleazy neighborhoods where bars and dives drew the restless damned, sashaying up and down the unlit streets luring men to lay with and rob.

Mardie refilled her teacup. She wrinkled her nose just thinking about Molochs. There was no trash service in Hell, forcing everyone to cart their rubbish to the dump where the Molochs burned it. The ugly dwarf-sized brutes had filthy dreadlocks and wild beards, and smelled worse than the garbage. Though she despised the Molochs, she could limit her contact with them. Not so with the Nergal demons.

Resembling the wide-eyed, rolly polly cherubs that dotted medieval Gospel parchments, they were, in fact, little monsters, insinuating themselves into the dreams of the damned, conjuring fearful images of broken teeth, gouged eyes, crushed toes, sliced off ears—all the things that had terrified her as a child. And, by God, they still terrified her, making her cry out, and forcing her to sleep with the lights on. There was nothing to be done about Nergals, and though they were truly rotten little shits, they couldn't ruin one's *real* life like the top-tier demons could.

The Balamms ran the banks, charging such spectacular interest that many of Hell's occupants preferred to deal with the black market Mob, mostly Sicilian priests who'd cut their teeth working at the Vatican Bank. For true greed and avarice, however, no one outshown the Mammons. They managed Hell's stock exchange, manipulating the market and bilking investors out of their money. Yet when things went south on rare, unanticipated occasions, they appealed to Satan for bailouts, which they unfailingly received. A stock market too bad to fail. Thoths were in charge of Hell's Internal Revenue Service. Yes, Virginia, death and taxes were forever. For those who couldn't pay, the Thoths took a real pound of flesh, leaving tax delinquents pitted with cantaloupe baller holes in their tummies, buttocks, and even breasts.

Last and worst, Shapeshifters were the top dogs of Satan's minions. Though mainly sent to Earth to disrupt the straights, they appeared in Hell as well, wearing the visage of your ex-spouse, ex-parent, or ex-whoeverthefuckmostembarrassed you, shouting out your secrets, broadcasting in squalid detail the deeds that landed you down here, while everyone watched. Goddam. What a place to live. Forever.

Chapter One

Mardie shook her head. Whatever the devils and demons did or didn't do, the fact was none of them could be killed. Which meant that the only real candidates down here for homicide were Hell's damned, and damned if they weren't already dead. Murder in Hell? Mardie shook her head and wished that she hadn't answered that phone call.

She got up, rinsed out her cup, drained the teapot, then scrubbed and dried them both.

Her mood had become truly foul. She knew she'd brought it on herself by wallowing in the humiliations and tortuous things that demons did to humans down here. Her conversation with the bastard demon pranking her had only been the start. Her horrible mood rendered her unsuitable for just about any activity she could think of. No, wait, she thought, with a grim smile. It was actually the perfect frame of mind for grocery shopping. She hated that chore more than any other obligation down here. Why not gird up her resentment and head out for the market? She was in just the right place to throw back any insults from the devils that ran the food stores. Where there's a mood, there's a way.

Mardie hung up her robe and changed into street clothes. She slipped on a bra and panties, a pair of white shorts, a pink tank top, and red leather sandals. Murder in Hell. She still couldn't get that out of her mind. You couldn't murder the Boss. You couldn't murder the henchmen. And you couldn't murder the humans. Mardie stepped out of her house. There was no way that murder was ever going to happen down here. Whatever despicable things Hell could be, it was, ironically enough, murder-proof.

Chapter Two

MARDIE STEPPED ONTO HER PORCH. The sky looked the same as it ever did, a lifeless, lead-colored monochrome gray. It was as if the Devil had ripped off Caesar's Palace's artificial indoor sky and adjusted the color, contrast, and brightness to corpse gray. It was also hot. Really, really hot.

Hell's suburbs flowed seamlessly in all directions, reaching all the way to the city core, a cluster of skyscrapers visible in the distance. The infernal burbs were composed of one-and two-story houses, shoulder-to-shoulder board and brick, rambling without any particular plan into the horizon. Only burnt-out yards and trashed vacant lots interrupted the monotony. Houses were in terrible shape. Paint was blistered, roofs were damaged, windows were boarded, and shattered glass lay strewn all over the sidewalks.

What little cheer there was in these dire surroundings was found in its human population. The neighborhood streets were busy with folks out and about, wearing skimpy shorts and loud tee shirts, tube tops and bikinis of all shapes and indecent sizes, fancy sandals or top of the line athletic shoes, and just about everyone seemed glad to be doing something outdoors. Could have been San Diego except there wasn't any ocean anywhere.

Chapter Two

Some people were riding bikes and some were walking. Everyone appeared to be happily focused on his or her particular task, which amazed Mardie. To her, Hell was just as meaningless as life on Earth had been. Folks there kept busy with this and that crap activity, convinced that movies and smart phones grounded them in a cool and enviable life situation. Mardie knew that was all seriously useless shit. There *and* here. Yet everyone was staying busy. She shook her head, pulled her front door shut, and walked down the steps.

She joined the stream of pedestrians on the sidewalk. She'd never been a big fan of walking, but there weren't a whole lot of other options if you had to go somewhere. Almost no one owned a car, taxis were expensive, and there was no public transportation. Mardie had been told that the rusty iron tracks embedded in the surface of many city streets had been laid for streetcars once upon a time. Never serviced, they had inevitably broken down and ceased running long ago. Mardie didn't actually know if that story was true. There were a lot of tales in Hell, and most of them were exaggerations or outright lies.

A pair of young females pedaled past her on a tandem bike. They were wearing red spandex suits with long sleeves and pant legs. Mardie thought they had to be insanely uncomfortable, but seeing their faces as they shot by, it was obvious the women knew they looked stylin' and *that's* all that mattered. In a place where everything was breaking or broken, hot and suffocating, manipulated in every possible way, stuffed with devils and damned humans, looking good, if only for the briefest moment, was the one solitary thing in Hell worth that last degree of discomfort.

Mardie sighed. *She* didn't look good and that bothered some immature part of her that she didn't. She thought that the veins on her hands were large enough to ship natural gas. The skin on her legs quivered when she walked and sagged when she stopped. She refused to look at her arms, and tried not to think about her face, lined by fags, pitted by booze, and sucked down by gravity and age. Oppressed by the full weight of her feminine decay, Mardie tripped. She scrambled to keep from falling and managed to stay upright. Breathing a sigh of relief she went on, keeping her eyes on the sidewalk, which she should have been doing all along. It was chipped and cracked, and there were gaps where chunks of cement had broken off. Holes pockmarked the surfaces, and there were long stretches where no sidewalk was left at all, just dirt and debris, an urban no-man's-land.

Mardie fell in with a group of seniors who were heading in the direction of the grocery store.

Most walked with crutches, or canes, or walkers. How did they get their groceries home? There were no volunteers to help. What little neighborliness there was down here was mostly aimed at getting laid. She watched a hunchbacked woman in a frayed fuchsia sundress approaching from the other direction. She had a large backpack strapped over the top of her misshapen spine. Her face was etched with pain. Sweat ran down her neck and soaked her dress. Mardie stepped aside to let the crone go by. If a person wanted consideration, they should have gone to Heaven. Down here you were on your own. The old woman knew it. Everyone knew it. And why should things be any different? This place was full of sinners. The weak may have inherited the Earth, but the selfish had inherited Hell.

A crowd had gathered outside Hells Bells Supermarket. Mardie stood up on her tiptoes and looked over the sea of white-haired heads. The store's automatic entry doors weren't operating. Employees were trying to get the doors to function, and since she had already risked her bones to get here, Mardie decided she could wait.

Chapter Two

Mardie realized that she knew the elderly man standing in front of her. He sported a cloud of salt-and-pepper hair that appeared to be occasionally combed but rarely cut. Despite the heat, he had on a blue wool sweater and brown corduroy pants. Mardie had met him at her neighborhood book club, one of the few social gatherings in Hell, and had, in fact, chatted with him on several occasions about their reading assignments. She reached out and touched him gently on the shoulder.

"Dr. Einstein?" she asked.

The old man turned all the way around and stared at her.

"Yes?" he answered, squinting at her.

"Dr. Einstein, it's Mardie."

The man cocked his head and scrutinized her. Sometimes Einstein, the possessor of possibly the greatest mind in the annals of scientific inquiry, thought that she was Helene, his housekeeper when he taught at Princeton.

"Hello, Mardie," he said. "How are you?"

"Still in Hell," she answered.

Einstein chuckled, and nodded his head. "That does sort of sum everything up, doesn't it?" He chuckled again, emitting a series of chirps, almost like hiccups. Why exactly Einstein had been damned was still a controversial topic among the demons. The most popular guess laid the blame on his advocacy of atomic bombs. President Franklin Roosevelt had found his arguments for their development persuasive and had built the bombs. His successor, Harry Truman, had used them on the Japanese cities of Hiroshima and Nagasaki. A couple of hundred thousand men, women, children, cats, and dogs were blown up, vaporized, and/or burned to a crisp. Thus, Hiroshima and Nagasaki were turned to bacon. Albert wound up down here. So did Frank and Harry.

The Wickett Sisters in Hell

Mardie was surprised that Einstein was at the market at all. He was one of Satan's greatest prizes and the Lord of Hell had assigned a platoon of devils to provide for his every need and whim.

"Dr. Einstein, what brings you here?" she asked.

Einstein glanced around furtively, then answered, speaking almost at a whisper.

"I came to buy tobacco. The Hausgeists always promise to bring me some, but they never do." Einstein's eyes narrowed and burned with anger. "I've decided that they buy it and then smoke it themselves."

The brilliant man shook his head, amazed that he was being robbed by his own minions. Furrows as craggy as Martian canals appeared on his forehead. Mardie couldn't be sure whether Einstein's irritation stemmed from being cheated, or because he was being denied tobacco. What *was* clear, however, was that he was fed up with being shortchanged. She watched the professor reach into his pants pocket and draw out a long black pipe fitted with a Meerschaum bowl. The soft, creamy stone was carved into the shape of a mermaid, with her tail curled up against her bottom and her arms wrapped around her breasts.

"Get that down here?" Mardie asked.

"Why, yes," Einstein answered, holding the pipe up for Mardie to see. "It was a welcome gift from Lucifer himself. I brought it because I'm going to smoke a pipeful the minute I get in that store."

"Good for you," Mardie encouraged.

Einstein nodded, appreciating Mardie's support, then put the pipe back in his pants pocket. As far as Mardie knew, there was no store regulation prohibiting smoking on the premises. Probably wasn't even a rule forbidding stealing tobacco right off the shelf. Hell, it was Hell.

Chapter Two

The crowd outside the market began to move forward. Mardie stood up on her toes again and looked. The supermarket doors had come to life.

"Well, good-bye Mardie," Dr. Einstein told her. He turned away and headed off in search of his tobacco. Mardie watched him go, shuffling away like the Little Tramp. Mardie went her own way, in search of Camemfaux cheese made from flour, and gluten-filled English muffins. Of course, the chances of acquiring either one of those staples were minuscule. It was much more likely she'd find artificially-flavored cheese spread and brown-and-serve rolls. Not that she would take such things home. If she were willing to eat that kind of crap, she would have moved to the States long before she'd died.

Chapter Three

Just as Mardie had expected, slim pickings had resulted from her search of Hells Bells. The Camemfaux was desiccated, at least two magnitudes beyond any acceptable age for fake cheese. The English muffins were stale and hard as volcanic tufa, but packages of brown-up rolls were stacked as tall as a shopper. Mardie had covered her eyes and moved on.

She foraged long enough to collect a bunch of wilted leeks, a dozen sprouting potatoes, four cans of spam that weren't swelling at the seams culled from a pile of cans that were, three eggs without cracks or foul smells, and several packages of granola. Funny how that last item was almost always available. One would have thought there'd be more Californians down here. She also found some soft, spotted apples that would make acceptable apple sauce or apple muffins, a few packages of raisins, and several different kinds of preserved curries in sealed jars. All in all, the foods she took home were usable, if not particularly fresh. Of course there was no meat. There was no prohibition against it. It was just never available, though rumors persisted that demons ate all kinds of domesticated animals, had full-scale charnel houses operating to meet demand, and that beefsteaks or a rack of lamb could

Chapter Three

be purchased on the flourishing black market run by devils and sprites of all descriptions.

As Mardie pushed her cart toward the checkout, smoke alarms went off all over the store. Batibat security demons, beefy Tongan female deities, looking like swollen ticks in their black robes, ordered shoppers to exit. Fire was fire, and as homely and broken down as Hell was, it was not fireproof. Mardie spun her cart around and went looking for Dr. Einstein. She didn't find him, but she did spot thick gray spirals of smoke wafting lazily above a corner of the store. Mardie grinned and then headed for the checkout. The mathematician had apparently been more lucky in his hunt for a smoke than she'd been in her quest for cheese.

The phone rang while she was putting her groceries away at home. She paused and stared at it. Two phone calls in one day? Unusual and unwelcome. She got calls now and then from her on-again, off-again paramour (or f-buddy, as he preferred to call himself, inadvertently grading his periodic performances as well). There was also an occasional misdial, but this morning's crank call was a first. All she could think was that the same obnoxious devil was calling her again. The phone kept ringing until her curiosity got the better of her worry. She reached down and picked up the receiver.

"This is Mardie."

"Mardell Wickett?" asked the all-too-memorable baritone voice. "We were somehow disconnected during our earlier conversation."

"Yes, I noticed that, too." Duh.

There was a long pause on the other side of the line. Was the suspicious demon sifting her words for nuance? Probably not that smart, Mardie decided.

"So what was your name again?" she asked.

The Wickett Sisters in Hell

"I told you before that my name was not important, Ms. Wickett." The demon was firm about remaining anonymous. "Suffice it to say that I work for Lord Lucifer."

"Suffice it, shit. I want to know your name."

Mardie was sure she heard a distinct growl on the other end of the line.

"I am a Samn demon," the caller answered, "a Central Asian demigod lately in the service of Tamerlane of Samarkand."

"You're saying that you're a demigod?" Mardie rebutted. "Smacks of a bureaucrat putting on airs, if you ask me."

"Putting on airs?" the Samn hollered into Mardie's ear. "How about if I come to your house and introduce myself by gnawing off one of your legs?"

Mardie dropped the receiver. Her tongue went numb and she felt dizzy. She had clearly way overstepped her place. The stooge on the line was actually a real stooge. Holy shit. Mardie's underarms soaked instantly. Bending down, she picked up the receiver and steeled herself.

"Well?" demanded the Samn devil.

"I'd prefer not," Mardie stuttered, hands shaking and mind panicking.

"Ha!" the Samn roared. "You'd prefer not. Good choice. Today at 3:00 p.m. you will present yourself at the Master's downtown office," he said, recovering his temper and bureaucratic demeanor.

"I'll be there," Mardie whispered.

"Of course you will."

"One last thing?"

"What?"

"Actually, it's nothing," she blurted out and hung up. "Oh, Christ," she said, horrified, and stared at the receiver sitting in the

Chapter Three

hook. She'd hung up on the Samn demon *twice*!! He'd probably chew off *both* her legs when he saw her.

Mardie sat down in a kitchen chair until her shakes went away. Then she fixed some tea and worried about why Satan could possibly want to see her. At least she wouldn't have to wait long to find out. Her doom was clearly appointed for 3:00 p.m. this very day.

She changed into a white blouse, tan slacks, and black flats, grabbed a navy blazer, and called for a taxi to take her downtown. A faded green '55 Chevy arrived late and honked outside her door. Viva Cuba, Mardie thought, seeing the vintage wreck pulled up at the curb. Out she went to her appointment with Lucifer, as fully convinced that she was innocent of trespass as Jacques de Molay was, only to find himself apprehended and dispatched by the French king on a Friday the thirteenth, thereby stamping that day and date as perennially unlucky. Mardie was probably fortunate that she had missed the fact that today was also Friday the thirteenth. God have mercy.

She was driven to a very old area of the city where the architecture looked like it had been designed for a Charles Dickens novel. The cabbie dropped her at a narrow two-story building that appeared both old and odd. It had a brick façade with French windows and an iron rod protruded over the door with a sign that read *Scrooge and Scratch*. Mardie supposed that to be a bit of devilish humor, for there had never been a real Scrooge, except, perhaps, Dickens himself. Abandoning his wife and family, he took up with a tawdry mistress, fathered a child, and then dumped them as well. No surprise that he was down here, too.

Mardie pulled open the front door and went in. It was hot outdoors, but the office was chilly, a frosty breeze blowing from a large air conditioner in the back. It was the first air conditioner Mardie had seen in Hell. Not even Hells Bells's dairy case had refrigeration. But then, it didn't have much dairy either.

Gray metal desks dotted a vast hardwood floor, each with a young clerk perched in front of a computer monitor. They were all bloody serious, eyes narrowed, foreheads wrinkled, fingers traversing their keyboards at great speeds. She supposed they were demons, another clutch of Satan's helpers, yet perhaps not. Anyone who'd ever had any dealings with demons knew they were lazy malingers, mean-spirited tricksters, vicious gossips, and as she had herself experienced just this morning on the phone, bullies. These chaps, on the other hand, were actually working hard, which meant, more likely than not, that they were humans, after all. Yet they were so young, Mardie thought. Investment bankers?

None of the clerks looked at her. Why should they? There was nothing special about her. She was not rich or famous, and she was not young. She was thankful that her occasional paramour still found her desirable. He wasn't a handsome man, but he was funny and always happy to hitch a ride with her to the land of *la petit morte*. A somewhat amusing turn of phrase, she thought, considering that they both lived in the land of *la grand morte*.

Behind an executive metal desk in the rear of the office sat the principal himself, scrutinizing his own computer monitor. Mardie had never seen the Devil before. He didn't look at her, but she couldn't stop staring at him. His hair was a mass of golden curls cascading over his shoulders. His skin was pale and smooth, his eyes icy blue, and his lips thin and masculine. The devil was Albrecht Durer. Or at least he had his face, which, Mardie thought, raised some prickly theological questions given that the world-famous artist had vociferously supported Luther's revolt against Catholic Rome. Screw that, Mardie thought. Lucifer was beautiful. Who cared about the rest?

Chapter Three

"Hello," he said, spotting her. His voice was soft and gentle.

"Have I the pleasure of addressing Ms. Mardell Wickett?" Satan looked at her attentively, then stood and gently beckoned to her. His manner seemed less like Hell's tyrant than some choirboy flirting from the recesses of a cathedral.

Mardie walked back and offered her hand. The Devil shook it gently.

"You *are* Mardell Wickett?" he asked, again.

"Yes, sir," she answered. Though Satan had called her Mardell twice, she was not in the least inclined to correct him as she had his agent earlier.

"Please call me Lucifer," the Devil told her, "and do you prefer Mardell or Mardie?"

"Anything will do," she responded, not able to take her eyes off Satan's face.

"Thank you for coming, Mardie," Lucifer replied, studying her for a moment. "How are things for you here?"

"I have no complaints." And she didn't. Nothing beyond daily inconveniences. Hell itself had turned out to be a somewhat less miserable existence than she'd had as a mortal.

"How do you stay busy?" Lucifer asked.

"I write," she replied.

"Did you write in your Earthly life?"

"I was a poet."

"A poet?" Lucifer murmured. He arched an eyebrow and observed Mardie with a curious stare.

"Yes."

"My. How in the world did you make ends meet?"

"I was also a traffic enforcement clerk."

Satan nodded.

19

"Down here I publish to a small but loyal group of readers."

"And you make money?"

"Enough to decorate my house the way I like."

"Good for you. Do you have any relatives down here?"

"I don't really know. My mother and father are dead. I have one sister, a nonidentical twin. She may still be alive for all I know."

"Do you miss her?"

"About as much as the emphysema that did me in."

Lucifer's eyes twinkled. "I never had siblings, unless you count other angels, but I understand exactly what you are saying. What did, or does, your sister do?"

"She's a homicide detective at Scotland Yard."

Lucifer looked pleased. "And her name?"

"Milicent."

Satan looked pleased. "Ah. She is, then, *that* Wickett. I am told that she is quite celebrated for her work."

For a single-minded, overbearing bitch who'd ignored her for fifty years, yes, her sister had done well. Mili Wickett had become a household name throughout the British Isles for solving a string of high-profile homicides across the kingdom.

"That would be my sister," Mardie answered at last.

"Brilliant," Lucifer said. "She's not here, by the way. So she's either still alive or . . . " Lucifer paused, and then pointed his index finger skyward.

"Up in Heaven," Mardie finished for him. Well, why not? She was a professional do-gooder.

"I'm sure we'll be able to locate her," Lucifer said. "We are in need of her talents as much as Scotland Yard ever was." The Devil paused and frowned. His face turned stiff and deadly serious. "Somehow, someway, someone in Hell has been murdered."

Chapter Three

Even though Mardie had heard it already, it was all the more stunning hearing it from Satan himself. How could it possibly be true? But it had to be true. Lucifer himself had just confided it. She shook her head, feeling dizzy and confused.

"I can't believe it," she whispered.

"And I would rather not," Lucifer replied grimly. "But it's true nonetheless, and I can think of no better detective to solve it than your sister." Lucifer looked at Mardie. "I need you as well. There is a role that *only you can play.* It is why I asked you here today."

"I'll do anything I can to help," Mardie answered.

"I am working on bringing your sister here. Negotiations have only just begun, but I have reason to be optimistic. Your role is to assist me in making her feel welcome and comfortable. I would like you to open your home to her for the duration of her stay."

Mardie's jaw dropped. *Welcome* the sister who for fifty years had succeeded in forgetting that she even had a twin? Make that person *comfortable* by inviting her into my own home? Mardie thought. Really? No, really?

Chapter Four

MARDIE DIDN'T KNOW HOW SHE COULD POSSIBLY come to grips with her impending doom. She, the twin who had miserably failed, had been asked by the ruler of Hell to shelter and serve the twin who had brilliantly succeeded. How could that ever be possible given a history of ill will and bad behaviors spanning fifty years?

Their mother had been a dedicated sugar addict, who had, in fact, introduced her newborns to sweets as soon as they could suck on sticks of hard candy held in their tiny fists. Mardie was horrified by how the sugar burned her tongue, but Mili overcame that painful introduction to refined sweets and proceeded to greedily devour every chocolate, caramel, marzipan, frosted nut, and marshmallow treat she was given. She and her doting mother quickly formed a codependent bond that celebrated the sweet life, a relationship that eventually and inevitably excluded Mardie, forcing her as a young child to deal with the reality that not only was her sister throwing her over, but her mother was as well. She fought this double heartbreak with every emotional tool at her disposal—crying, begging, arguing, refusing to eat or sleep or talk—the results of which only succeeded in disgusting her twin and outraging her mother.

Chapter Four

When Mardie finally accepted the fact that she'd been cut out of both of their lives, she began looking for solace elsewhere. Long before she entered senior school, she was smoking and snorting and blowing boys in the loo, and what little time she spent in class resulted in disciplinary warnings for poor attitude, late work, and failing marks, all of which simply confirmed that she was a loser.

Mardie debauched her way to graduation, earning the stains on her clothing and her reputation. Her vocational exam score was so low she qualified for but a single position, a bottom-of-the-barrel secretarial job sorting and filing traffic tickets in Kensington. She took it. Unable to afford a place to live anywhere in the pricey neighborhood where she worked, she began a twice-a-day eighteen kilometer tube commute back and forth to Slough, where she lived in a windowless flat filled with cast-off furniture from a local thrift shop.

Thus she lived and worked for forty years, going gray, then bottled blond, spending her free hours smoking, drinking, and collecting lovers. Like Easter eggs, she discovered them in pubs, sports stadiums, and other women's bedrooms. She also found brief respite from her unhappy existence writing poetry, providing comfort not only to herself, but also to a tiny cultlike group of followers whose own crucified existences fed on her tortured stanzas of a life misspent.

Meanwhile, Mili prospered. Perhaps as a result of her endless childhood quests to stalk the perfect sweet, Mili developed an ability to track down lawbreakers with equal dedication, and not just run-of-the-mill criminals who'd offed a spouse, robbed a merchant, or smuggled an illegal drug, but the perverse and evil creatures who poisoned children's aspirin, mailed anthrax to pensioners, and butchered up local vicars for fresh ground round.

Mili pursued the dark and dangerous trails of such monsters with exuberant passion, her delight in the chase exceeded only by her satisfaction in seeing the fiends captured or killed in the attempt to do so. Her record of success was such that she rapidly topped the storied histories of former Yard champions, then trampled their accomplishments into the dust.

Mardie saw Mili's pictures splashed all over the tabloids and, while she begrudgingly acknowledged her twin's success, she also observed with no small satisfaction that over the years Mili's figure ballooned far beyond the girth of their severely overweight mother. Mardie felt no pity for the cow, any sisterly concern having been squeezed out eons ago by the bitter contempt she held for her twin.

So, these were the histories of Mardie and Milicent, their lives sundered by maternal favoritism, then permanently divided by disdain, by time, and ultimately by death itself, surely not the stuff to support Lucifer's hope that Mili would ever consent to stay with Mardie, or for that matter that Mardie would ever invite her to cross her threshold.

Despite recognizing all of these issues, Mardie knew that Mili would probably agree to work on Lucifer's case, even if it meant having to stay with her sister. Perversely, she might even welcome such an occasion, seizing it as an opportunity to gloat over Mardie's butchered life and eternal demise. Now wouldn't that be swell? Her life ruined again, and by the same terrible twin.

Lucifer rang Mardie the following morning.

"Yes, sir?" she answered, seeing Lucifer's image on her monitor. She had slept poorly. The face of the demon-in-charge staring at her now had also stared at her all night long in her dreams.

Chapter Four

"Good morning, Mardie," Lucifer said. "Is your webcam on? I can't see you at all."

"Yes, it is. I can see you fine."

"Your camera is not working," the Devil said, irritated. "I'll send someone over to fix it."

Mardie watched as Satan summoned a minion. A thin man in horned-rim spectacles and a tie-dye tee shirt with *Woodstock* printed on it appeared and was immediately dispatched to repair her webcam. Lucifer turned back to Mardie.

"And how are you?" he asked, distinctly pleased at being able to order somebody around, whatever the reason. My, Mardie thought. There once was a little boy with a curl in the middle of his forehead.

"I am fine, thank you," she answered. She'd almost said she was well, but that word had little meaning for the dead and the damned.

"Have you written any new poems lately?"

Mardie was so surprised by Lucifer's question she almost dropped the phone receiver.

"No, actually."

"Sometime I would enjoy reading some of them," Lucifer said.

Mardie was so taken aback tears came to her eyes. "I would be honored," she finally managed to gasp. "Thank you."

"I have some updates on your sister, Milicent," Satan said, choosing not to deal with Mardie's emotional reaction. He could handle *human conditions* in poems, but dealing with them in person went far beyond his interest in Mardie or any other person in Hell. "She passed three years ago from diabetic complications."

Dead from diabetes, Mardie thought. What a surprise.

"She died heroically, however, using her last hours to flush out an assassin who had murdered England's Assistant Minister of Meat Procurement." Mardie raised her eyebrows. Lucifer couldn't see

Mardie, but he sensed her ambivalence. "Perhaps not Her Majesty's most important civil servant," he went on, "but for Mili to pin down his killer, *even* while she lay on her deathbed, was a triumphant way for her to conclude her career *and* her life."

"I don't know what to say," Mardie mumbled. Nothing nice came to mind, even for the Minister of Meat Procurement.

"She went to Heaven, no surprise. Naturally I would have preferred that Milicent was already down here and readily available to help, but since she is not I shall have to get Jehovah's approval for her participation."

"He can't want a murderer on the loose any more than you, can He?"

Lucifer shrugged. "I don't rightly know. He doesn't express much interest in this place. In fact, He's never been here, not even once."

"Maybe He doesn't need to come. I mean, He *is* omniscient."

"As in, knows all, sees all?" Lucifer clarified.

Mardie nodded.

"Not a chance," Lucifer uttered, miffed. "That's propaganda dreamed up by His toadies on Earth. He hasn't a clue what has happened here. I'll have to explain it when I see Him, and *then* make my pitch for Mili's involvement. I just hope I can get away before He launches into one of His endless discussions about who's gone to Heaven recently and who wound up in Hell."

"Because He doesn't know."

"Actually, because He does. It's confusing, but when it comes to souls, He's always up-to-date."

"Lost sheep?"

"Lost bet."

"You mean there really is a competition between you two?"

Chapter Four

Mardie had never been to church, but everyone had heard about God and Satan going neck and neck to win souls.

"Yes, but if I may tell you confidentially, He's so far behind now it has humbled Him a little." So much for the neck and neck, thought Mardie. "The last couple of times I saw Him, He even called me Lu. I think it's His way of trying to get past an old problem we had."

"You mean the rebellion of the angels?"

"Where did you hear that?" Lucifer demanded, instantly furious. His cheeks turned crimson and his eyes blazed bright as shooting stars.

"I don't know," she whispered, withering under Satan's wrath. "Some book."

"Well, you didn't read it in the Bible, because it's not *in* the Bible. Rebellion of the angels?" Lucifer was shouting now. Then like an exploding Roman candle, his hair lit on fire, flames flaring out like Medusa's snakes, and his face creased with fury. "There were no angels! It was me, just me, and it wasn't a rebellion. It was an *assassination*."

"Oh my God!" Mardie gasped.

"You can relax," Lucifer said and held up his hand. "I failed." Like a meteor plunging into deep space, his fiery aura flamed out and his appearance returned to normal, except for his eyes, which still flickered with anger. "It was a long time ago. Right now we both have to get ready for Mili."

Mardie didn't answer. Lucifer had tried to murder Jehovah. She couldn't even begin to wrap her head around that. On the other hand, maybe it was just a lie. Satan seemed to have a history of that, after all. Still, assassinate God?

"Are you still there? I can't see you, remember?"

"I'm here," Mardie answered, paying attention again. Maybe not enough attention, however, because what she said next was the wrong thing to the wrong person. "I've been thinking a lot about it, and I don't think Mili should stay with me."

Satan's eyes narrowed to slits and he ground his teeth so loudly Mardie shrank back from the monitor.

"What happened to 'I'll do anything I can to help?'" Satan asked, struggling to control himself. "You *do* understand why I need Mili, right?"

"I do," Mardie answered meekly.

"Well, let me remind you, anyway. Someone's body was tossed on my front steps," Lucifer spit out, little tongues of flame sprouting on top of his head, "gutted and beheaded."

"Gutted?" Mardie choked on the word.

Satan nodded, flames engulfing his locks once again. "Bloody well butchered!"

"Do you know who the dead person is?"

"Not a clue. I need Mili to find out who dumped that corpse at my place so I can wreak havoc on him. Are you going to help me, or not?" There weren't any nuances in the Devil's voice. He was demanding that Mardie capitulate. Now.

"I will do whatever you want," Mardie vowed. "I must tell you, though, Mili and I do not get along."

"You don't have to get along!" Lucifer shouted. "I want *her* taken care of and I want *you* to do it."

"I will," Mardie cried. "I'll take care of her every moment she's here. Not just at home, but wherever she goes and whatever she does."

"*What did you just say?*" Lucifer responded, annunciating each word with excruciating precision.

"I said, I will stay by her side the whole time she is here," Mardie repeated.

Chapter Four

Lucifer leaned forward and stared at what he hoped was Mardie's terrified face.

"Do you mean it?"

"I do."

"Don't forget you said that," Lucifer said, speaking so softly it almost sounded like a hiss. "Don't ever forget." Then without another word he was gone.

Mardie jumped up out of her chair, shook her fists in the air, and yelled every four letter word she could think of. Why had she promised that she would stick to Mili? She'd rather spend time with the headless, gutless dead man than with her sister. It was pure fear that had prompted her insane promise, she knew that, and now that the terrifying conversation with Lucifer had ended, the experience overwhelmed her. She dropped down onto a chair and began shaking violently. The Devil sounded like he could gut her and rip *her* head off. She'd never been so terrified in her life. It took fifteen minutes before she could breathe normally, and fifteen more before she could get up and put on the teakettle.

Chapter Five

THAT NIGHT THERE WAS A KNOCK on Mardie's front door. She thought it might be her lover at long last. She flipped on the porch light and looked through the peephole, a precaution she had just begun now that a murderer was on the loose. The porch was still dark. She flicked the light switch up and down a few times but the bulb didn't come on. Naturally. Her caller flipped on a flashlight and revealed himself.

It was a demon, and not just a run-of-the-mill demon, either. It was a Shapeshifter, the kind of demon Lucifer used to torment both the quick and the dead, appearing in the guise of lost loves, fearful enemies, dead relatives, whatever apparition was guaranteed to make the victim truly miserable. The morph outside Mardie's door was seven foot tall. It was purple. It was Barney the Dinosaur.

"Hello!" he told her. "I can see you looking through the peephole! Why don't you open the door?"

Mardie did.

"What do you want?"

"Are you Mardie Wickett? Resident here for three years, seven weeks, and thirteen days?"

"What about the hours and the minutes?"

Chapter Five

"Eight hours, six minutes, *and* twelve seconds," the demon added cheerfully.

"Well, superdeedooper. Why are you here? There must be some reason that you've picked me to irritate."

"The Master said to tell you that your sister has been granted a leave from Heaven to assist him. She will be arriving tomorrow—"

"And to make sure that my house is in order," Mardie finished.

Barney looked hurt at being interrupted. "Well, not really. The Master says that she will be taken to a hospital down here."

"A hospital? What's wrong with her?"

"She's not well."

That set Mardie back. Mili had gone to Heaven. How could she be ill? Wasn't everything supposed to be perfect there? No more sorrow, no more tears, no more diabetes?

"Fine," she told the waiting dinosaur. She'd sort out her thoughts later when he wasn't hovering over her. "You've delivered your message, now leave."

The demon cocked his large purple head and looked at her.

"Do you want to know more about the corpse on the Master's steps?" He winked knowingly. "I've seen it."

"You? Why you?"

Not replying, Barney split open his stomach. Guts spewed out like a garbage disposal in reverse. Mardie stepped back, disgusted.

"The victim was missing all of those," the demon said, pointing at the steaming offal on Mardie's steps. "And this." The top of Barney's head flipped open like a jack-in-the-box and out shot his brain. It landed on Mardie's steps.

"Stop it!"

"But there's more!" He raised his hands and lifted off his head, then dropped it at his feet.

The Wickett Sisters in Hell

"I said stop it!" Mardie screamed.

Gutless and headless Barney sat down. He sagged, slowly collapsing on the steps. "This is exactly what the Master saw," his severed head reported.

Instantly the demon changed into the prone body of a short, slight man wearing an old-fashioned black suit. His white shirt was ripped open and the collar soaked in blood, but there was no head, and despite his belly being split up the middle there was no viscera. Mardie knew in an instant that this *was* exactly what Lucifer saw.

She threw up. Then she stepped back and slammed the door shut. She wiped off her mouth and washed her hands in the bathroom, then returned and put her eye to the peephole again. Barney was standing there, looking at her. He smiled and waved.

"Remember, I love you!"

"Go away!" Mardie yelled through the door. Barney waved again, then shuffled off humming, apparently satisfied with the success of his shitty little mission.

Mardie couldn't believe that Lucifer had authorized this barbaric display of protoplasmic horror. She'd call him, that's what she'd do. She'd call and report that lousy bastard. A morph couldn't just go around doing shit like this.

She opened the door. There was blood all over her front steps. Grumbling, she fetched a mop and a bucket and began to wipe it up. She kept seeing the gutted, headless body of the dead man lying on the steps while she mopped. Thank God Mili was coming to sort this out, she thought, then quickly tried to forget it, flushing that thought away as fast as she could. When she finished cleaning up the blood, she mopped up her vomit. What a night.

Chapter Five

She rinsed the mop, washed out the bucket, then put in a call to Lucifer. She got his answering machine, the old-fashioned kind that allowed the listener to screen calls for pests, in which category the Devil had already likely consigned her.

> Hi, You've reached Lucifer. I assume that the only way you could have this number is if I gave it to you. Let me warn you, that better be the case. Leave a message.

The machine beeped. Mardie left her message.

> This is Mardie Wickett. Your messenger told me that my sister will be hospitalized when she arrives. How can that be? She's from Heaven, right? I also think that the demon who delivered your message was an ass. You have my number.

Mardie hung up. Had she been too cheeky? It was, after all, the Lord of Hell she was addressing, and she'd seen what happened when he got pissed off. She tossed some kindling into the stove, filled the teakettle, and sat down. She couldn't get over that Mili was coming all the way here from Heaven only to check into a hospital. Mardie knew she was ignorant about what went on behind the Pearly Gates, but you didn't have to be Saint Peter's best friend to know that things weren't supposed to work like that. Wings, harps, and angels, but no diabetes. The teapot whistled, and Mardie took it off the stove. It crossed her mind that when it came to how things worked in Heaven, it probably wasn't her place to even ask Lucifer why Mili hadn't been healed up there. Not that it would stop her from asking again.

✳ ✳ ✳

Satan leaned back in his office chair, folded his hands on his chest, and looked at Mardie.

"Why does it matter that Mili was hospitalized when she arrived?" he asked. "Suffice it to say that she needed the care."

Lucifer had returned Mardie's call early in the morning, found that her phone camera had broken yet again, and asked her to come to his office instead. She did. He waved off her complaints about the shapeshifting demon. Who didn't like Barney? Mardie frowned and immediately started pressing for answers about Mili.

"She's from *Heaven*. Why should she need *any* kind of help?"

"Allow me to explain. As you've discovered, things in Hell are not so different from how they are on Earth. People get offended. People get angry. People still feel sad, and hurt, and lonely. And, just like on Earth, they try to blot out those feelings with even more powerful emotions like lust, envy, and jealousy, or they simply try to escape from them, with smoking, drinking, and drugs. There is, of course, no real escape, and when folks sober up they find themselves feeling just as lonely or sad or unhappy as they ever did, so they start the whole destructive cycle all over again."

Mardie felt a little like she was being lectured by Dr. Phil, and Lucifer was not finished.

"In Heaven things are different. Oh, folks still have the same emotions as here. They feel depressed, left out, unloved. But there people reach out to each other. They practice empathy, kindness, and forgiveness, and above all, love—and *these* emotions, pure and simple, heal the negative ones. So, Heaven is indeed, as you expected, about being healthy, *but it starts on the inside.*"

Chapter Five

Well, that was all well and good, Mardie thought. But nothing the Devil had said explained why Mili was ill in Heaven, why she was still sick here, and why she was lying in a hospital bed down here at this very moment.

Lucifer studied Mardie's face. He could tell his words had fallen on stony ground.

"For whatever reason, Mili *is* the way she is," he went on. "Why she was not been made whole in Heaven is not my concern nor, to be blunt, is it yours. Your task is to go and meet your sister and determine whether you two big girls can live together in the same house. *Your* house."

"Does she know I'm here?"

"If by *here*, you mean Hell, no, she does not."

"So I'm supposed to just show up and surprise her?"

"Yes, that's exactly what you're supposed to do," he shot back, his voice rising.

Mardie shrank back a bit, but did not yield.

"I'll go, but I'm not promising anything. I'll have to see how Mili treats me."

Satan's eyes turned to slits. Was he really hearing this woman sass him? The only thing that kept him from exploding was that she appeared to be leaving at last.

"I wouldn't be surprised if Milicent assumes the very same defensive posture as you," the Devil replied.

"I never did a thing to her."

"*Or* for her, *or* with her," Satan countered. "Isn't that equally true?"

Mardie didn't answer.

Satan stood up. It was time for Mardie to go.

"You have things to do, and lest you forget, so do I. There's a putrefying body still lying on the steps of my house."

"You left the corpse there?"

Lucifer put a hand on his hip and stared at her. "Don't you ever watch *CSI*?" Mardie shook her head. "The location where a murdered person's body is discovered is designated a *crime scene* by authorities," Satan explained. "Kept *undisturbed*, it may hold clues. Your sister needs to study the crime scene exactly the way I found it."

"Then you better hope," Mardie responded, standing up herself, "that Barney didn't go back there again last night."

Lucifer stared at her, puzzled. Mardie turned and walked out. Old maid in Hell, one. Satan, zero.

Chapter Six

THE HOSPITAL LOOKED LIKE A FORTRESS and smelled like a battle zone, the pungent odors of alcohol and antiseptics mixing with the sour smells of blood, gore, and decay. The only odor missing was the smell of death because no one died in this hospital, or any other hospital in Hell. Mardie walked toward the reception desk, working her way through a corridor packed with people waiting for help. Some were in wheelchairs, some were lying on gurneys, but most were sitting on the floor with their backs against the wall, bloody bandages on their arms, legs, chests, and heads. Mardie shook her head as she passed by. No one here would ever be the same again.

A senior citizen with blue hair and a pink uniform looked up at her when she finally reached the desk. She was wearing a badge that read *Volunteer Mei Wong*. Her face was as devoid of emotion as a Puritan gravestone angel.

"Broken, bleeding, or burned?" Mei Wong asked, without a discernible hint of empathy.

"I am here to see Milicent Wickett," Mardie replied.

The volunteer spun through an old-fashioned Rolodex card file. Mardie watched the elderly Chinese woman and noted the prominent gold crucifix hanging around her neck. It hadn't apparently done her much good, Mardie thought. Why in the world would she still be wearing it here?

"You are Mardell Wickett?" the volunteer asked, looking up from Milicent's card. Mardie nodded. "Your sister is on the fourth floor, Room A. The Master sent a car and the driver is waiting at the front entrance." The woman looked at Mardie. She didn't have any wrinkles on her forehead or lines around her mouth. Mei Wong didn't smile very often. Better than Botox.

"Thank you," Mardie told her. "Which way do I go?"

The receptionist pointed toward another crowded hallway, with more people waiting. Many wore soccer jerseys with team logos. Mardie recognized them. Manchester United and rival Manchester City fans had been at it again. Soccer players couldn't get along well enough in Hell to field teams, but their fans maintained the sport's larger traditions of mayhem and fisticuffs. There were black eyes and bleeding faces, bruises from bats and pipes, gashes and torn flesh from fists, cleats, and God knew what else. As Mardie made her way through the hall she noticed that everyone was waiting alone, suffering their ailments in solitude. There was no marriage in Hell, and there were no children. Mardie had never married or had any babies, and didn't regret that she hadn't, but it did make Hell quieter and sadder not to see married couples or kids.

The door to Room A was open. Mardie walked in without knocking. It was empty except for a single hospital bed. She stared at the person in it, a grossly rotund female with a red blotchy face and a blond bouffant hairdo. She had her eyes closed. If Mardie hadn't been told that Milicent Wickett was in this room, she would not have known that this woman was her twin. Once her sister had been a ringer for Meryl Streep. Not anymore. Barely a mote was left of the pretty young woman she'd been five decades ago.

Chapter Six

Mili opened her eyes and saw Mardie. She studied her for a moment.

"It *is* you, isn't it, Mardie?" she asked.

Mardie nodded.

"You look wonderful. It's hard to believe we're related. You, svelte with your Victoria's Secret boobs. Me, fat as a walrus, one foot in the grave."

Mardie stood embarrassed and confused. Mili noticed and smiled. She pulled up the blankets at the bottom of the bed and pointed. Her left foot had been amputated above the ankle.

Mardie opened her mouth to speak, but Mili raised her hand, grinning at her own joke.

"Please. It is how it is. My lack of self-control cost me my foot *and* my life." Mili sat up slowly and held out her hand to Mardie. She walked over to the bed and took it. It was soft and warm. She couldn't remember the last time she had held her sister's hand.

"Mardie, is this really Hell?" Mili's face was troubled. Mardie nodded. "I am so sorry," Mili whispered, "so sorry."

Mardie pulled her hand away. "I don't need your pity."

"I don't mean to be judgmental. I am just so surprised that you are here. You were a poet, sensitive and self-revealing, a faithful employee, and a doggedly loyal lover. Everything I ever learned about you bespoke a decent, humane person."

"Everything you learned?"

"I kept a distant eye on you, sister," Mili replied. "Forgive me for not telling you."

Mardie heard Milicent's apologetic words, but there was no repentance in her tone. She'd spoken in the exact same perfunctory official voice used by the police, judges, and counselors Mardie had been forced to deal with as a youthful lawbreaker. Any expression of concern or sympathy, and any spoken commitment to help that she had ever heard from one of them had only and always been a lie. And now it was her sister.

"Why would you check on me? Why would you want to know anything about me?"

"My motives were selfish, I'm afraid. I wanted to know that you were all right. And you were. But now I find you *here*."

Mardie didn't know how to respond. For fifty years her twin had not made a single effort to communicate with her, not even when their mother had died. *Yet Mili claimed she had been checking on her.* Mardie shivered involuntarily, as though her sister's *Geist* had passed through her soul unbidden. If that were true, where had she been when one of Mardie's so-called paramours beat her and robbed her and left her for dead? And how had she missed Mardie's crack overdose, when she'd been wrenched back to life only to be sentenced to three years in prison for possession? And perhaps most compelling of all, why had Mili failed to appear during Mardie's final weeks, bedridden and tethered to a hospital respirator while her emphysema stoppered up her remaining alveoli one by one.

Oh, stop bitching, you old bag, Mardie snapped at herself. You're dead, she's dead, who gives a flying fuck about what she did or didn't do? Yet looking again at Milicent, she realized that her sister still did care. She was patiently waiting for some expression of gratitude *for her snooping*!

"I'm sorry you wasted any time checking on me," Mardie said, her words graceless and her tone rude, "then or now."

Mili frowned at the rebuff. She stared at Mardie for a moment, as though waiting for her twin to apologize. It did not happen.

"Well, that's that, then," she remarked, seeming to rebound, but Mardie could tell by her frosty manner and her perfunctory tone

Chapter Six

that she'd felt stung. "I never interfered in your life and I don't intend to start now," Mili claimed, as disingenuously as any sibling who'd ever tried to defend an inappropriate action. "I have come here with but a single goal in mind, to solve this murder. Now let's go."

Mili pulled away her bed covers and stood up. She had on a taupe silk blouse, navy slacks, and a brown pump on her right foot. Her pants were pinned beneath the stump of her left leg.

"Please bring the wheelchair," she asked, and pointed to it across the room. "I hobble to and fro using a cane, but mostly I prefer the chair."

"It's okay for you to leave?" Mardie asked, choosing not to ask why Mili had been hospitalized in the first place.

"Yes," Mili said.

Mardie fetched the wheelchair and positioned it next to the bed. Mili reached down and flipped it around so it faced her, then grabbed both arms and with a quick, practiced movement spun herself around and dropped into the wheelchair. Mardie was astonished at her sister's upper body strength.

"Remind me not to piss you off," she said.

"Too late," she answered, gazing at her sister with the same ironic expression the jailer must have used when Marie Antoinette had asked for cake to eat since there was no bread.

So, Mardie thought, the niceties were over. The first conversation she'd had with her twin in half a century and the truce hadn't lasted even a few seconds. Shorter half-life than a male orgasm.

Mili pushed at the rubber wheels of the chair but it wouldn't move. One of the small wheels in front was stuck. She called the hospital operator and told her to get a working chair up to her room immediately. An orderly rushed in with a replacement almost before she'd hung up. Mardie stared at the man. He looked remarkably like

George W. Bush. He smiled at her, flashing the same wiseass grin that had made many people doubt the American Commander-in-Chief's mental acuity, Mardie included. She smiled back. Bush or not, it was good to see that the chap had found something he could handle.

Mili switched to the replacement chair, and they took the elevator to the lobby, where they exited the hospital toward the sleek black BMW waiting at the curb. The chauffeur, a slight, elderly man, stepped out with a grin. Mili smiled when she saw the driver, and greeted him by name.

"Well, well, well, Pfot," she said. "I should have expected to see you down here. How are you, dear boy?" The chauffeur was at least an octogenarian, with an abnormally thin build and a face that appeared to have sunken down onto the bones beneath. He nodded graciously and smiled a twisted smile, showing crooked teeth that were bad even by British standards. Mardie was not particularly surprised that Mili should have run into someone she knew down here. Probably had photographed the bugger herself for the Royal Mail's Most-Wanted displays.

"I'm doing well, Miss Wickett. Thank you for asking," Pfot responded to Mili's friendly greeting. His voice was youthful in contrast to his wreck of the Hesperus appearance. "I heard that you were coming to help the Master solve the awful problem he's run into."

"Well, I'll be working on it, at any rate," Mili replied modestly. Probably trying to avoid jinxing herself right out of the chute was Mardie's take. Mili eyed Pfot seriously. "I better not find out that you're somehow involved," she warned. Pfot grinned and didn't answer. Mili nodded toward her twin. "This is my sister, Pfot, Mardie Wickett. Mardie, a former associate, Paul Pfotenhauer."

"You were colleagues?" Mardie asked, even though her every instinct weighed in against the likelihood of that possibility. The

Chapter Six

skeletal old-timer had a rawboned manner about him that would have been completely unacceptable to the stuffy patricians running Scotland Yard.

Both Pfotenhauer and Mili guffawed loudly at Mardie's question.

"Pfot was a stoolie," her sister clarified. "*My* well-paid stoolie, until he was retired by the London mob."

"Oh my Lord," Mardie said. She had heard of men being knocked off by the criminal underground, but she had never come face-to-face with one of them.

"Never you mind, Miss," Pfot said, appreciating Mardie's pity. "I had a quick and painless leave-taking," he turned his neck and pointed to a neat bullet hole at the base of his skull, "which actually put me onto the first bit of good luck I'd had in a very long time. Right after I arrived here, the Master appointed me chauffeur for his personal visitors."

"I am so glad for you, Pfot," Mili said, clasping his shoulder and giving it an affectionate squeeze, "and truly delighted to see you, dear lad. Once again into the breach, eh?"

"More like into the BMW," Pfot answered, making Mili laugh.

"You always were a clever piece of shite."

Pfot opened the car doors for both women. Mardie got in while Mili stood up out of the wheelchair, balanced herself on her one foot, and carefully slid into the backseat next to Mardie.

"Pfot," Mili called up to the front of the car, "I want to see where the homicide was committed."

"Yes, Ma'am," Pfotenhauer said. He started the car, turned on the air conditioning, and pulled onto the street.

Mardie looked at her sister. "Do police ever refer to a homicide location as a *crime scene?*" she asked.

"Where did you hear that?"

"Lucifer used it."

"Did he take you there?"

"No, but a wiseass demon dicking with me morphed into the corpse on my front steps."

Mili eyed Mardie carefully.

"He actually imitated the dead body?"

"He claimed to have seen it."

"And what did *you* see?"

"I'm no expert."

"I'm not asking you to be an expert. I am asking you to tell me what you saw."

Mardie remembered all too clearly what she saw.

"The victim was headless," she began, visualizing the grotesque corpse lying on her front steps. Mardie's stomach growled, as though confirming the disturbing images in her head. She slipped her hand over her mouth, but her tummy settled down again.

"Was it male or female?"

"Male, and he was older. He had salt-and-pepper hair on his chest."

Mili looked surprised. "That's an impressive detail."

"His insides were missing, stomach, intestines, everything, just gone."

"Was there blood?"

"A lot of blood, but it came from his neck. The top of his suit and the collar of his white shirt were soaked with it, and after the demon left, there was blood on my steps."

"How did the neck tissue appear? Was it cut cleanly, or was there a roughness to the effort?"

Chapter Six

The neck had been horribly mutilated. Mardie's stomach rumbled again. She ignored it and answered.

"The skin was quite jagged. I remember thinking that it looked as if the man's head had just been wrenched away."

Mili frowned. "I don't think that's possible, even down here." She fell silent, thinking about what Mardie had shared. She murmured softly, and shook her head.

"What?" Mardie asked.

"I was just thinking out loud, sorry."

"That's okay. But could you think out loud just a little louder?"

Mili glanced at Mardie and gave her a wink. Mardie was grateful for that little bit of warmth, then immediately hated herself for needing it. This was a crime investigation, she reminded herself, not a reunion.

"I was thinking that the body must have been eviscerated prior to being transported to Lucifer's house," Mili answered, "hence, little or no bleeding from that area. The neck, on the other hand, did bleed, or at least drain, on the Devil's steps, indicating that the victim was very likely beheaded there. But why then and why there? A brutal afterthought? Perhaps, given the tearing of the flesh and spilled blood. A last minute souvenir?" Mardie let out an involuntary groan. Mili nodded. "Very possible, I'm afraid, and I've seen worse, believe me."

"How can you have all these possibilities to explore when you haven't even seen the corpse yet?"

"They're all tidbits from what *you* saw, ducks."

Mardie was surprised, yet secretly pleased, to be acknowledged.

"The important thing at the beginning of an investigation, however, is to ask questions about the clues, avoiding the temptation to form conclusions until much more about the crime has been discovered and analyzed. For example, despite the fact that the deceased chap is missing both his head *and* his innards, we must resist speculating that the murderer initially intended to kill him."

Mardie raised her eyebrows. Oh, right. The disfiguring and dissecting must have just gotten out of hand.

"Alternatively, the person who killed our victim may have intended from the beginning that his deed not only be lethal, but humiliating as well. Gutting the dead man? Cutting off his head? Dumping his body where it would be found by Hell's most famous occupant?" Mili paused for effect, then went on. "Smacks of *deliberate*, doesn't it? Yet the killer *took the head with him* when it would seem obvious that he would have left it behind so that Satan could see *exactly* who had been abandoned on his steps.

"Which raises another matter, how did the murderer get anywhere near the well-guarded estate of Lucifer, let alone make it all the way to his front door? Yet he did, apparently undetected and unnoticed. That feat, considering all of the preparation required to pull it off, was definitely not left to chance." Mili shook her head, entranced by the genius required to not only execute such a terrible crime on Satan's turf, but to have pulled it off right in front of his own home.

"My head hurts," Mardie complained.

Mili turned and looked at her. "Sorry, but all of this rousting about, this detecting if you will, sprang from your contribution. So many things to consider, and we haven't even arrived at the crime scene yet." Mili's eyes grew large with excitement. "Brilliant, what?"

"My head hurts," Mardie repeated.

Chapter Seven

Mili watched the urban landscape pass by as the BMW threaded its way out of the city. There were no trees, or flowers, or parks. Brown hills rolled on as far as she could see, covered with brick and tin shanties without number.

"Bleak," she commented. "A city without a soul."

"Filled with hundreds of millions of people," Mardie added.

"My," Mili responded. "Heaven is so spacious that I used to look around and wonder where everyone was. Now I know."

"They're all down here."

Mili grinned at her sister.

Mardie grinned back, then instantly felt self-conscious, as though she had somehow let down her guard.

Mili reached over and tapped Mardie's arm. "You're reconstituted from your own DNA and RNA, did you know that?"

Mardie shook her head.

"Whoever would have guessed that the religious busybodies haranguing about a physical resurrection would be right? One of them, perhaps even Saint Paul himself, went so far as to insist that believers would be given *two* bodies, one for their time on Earth, and one for their time in Heaven. Who knew?"

"You mention Heavenly and Earthly bodies, but what about my Hellish body?" Mardie pointed at her chest.

"*I'm* the one with the Hellish body," Mili answered. "You're the one with the tits and ass."

Mardie instantly blushed, startled by her sister's down-to-Earth remark.

Mili enjoyed seeing her sister's reaction. "I'm not always a boring old biddy. I will, however, probably always be a fat old biddy. In Heaven we eat and drink just like we did before so, true to form, I overeat and overdrink and crap my insides out just like before."

"It's the same here, though the food is appallingly second rate, stuffed with shitloads of added sugar and filler."

Mili snorted. "Shitloads?" she repeated, and laughed out loud.

Mardie laughed as well. "Yes, and when I do get around to needing the toilet, it's quite an ordeal."

Mili roared. "Rather ironic that your ordeals down here would be the same as the ones I experience in Heaven." Mili wiped her eyes and looked at Mardie.

"Where do you buy food around here? I haven't seen any grocers."

"We have supermarkets, and street trucks sell convenience food, hamburgers, hot dogs, tacos, and shawarma, all made out of tofu."

"Mystery meats."

"Pretty much."

"Remember that touristy little version of Chinatown in central London where we ate once? I swear that every dish we ordered came with some kind of mystery meat."

Chapter Seven

Mardie nodded, remembering. It had been just the sisters out together. They had barely ordered their food when the topic of their mother's sugar addiction came up. They proceeded to argue through dinner and all the way home on the bus, climaxing with a vicious attack by Mardie because of the favoritism their mother had showed Mili.

The sisters sat quietly for a few moments. Then Mili picked up the conversation again.

"There isn't any meat in Heaven, butchering is forbidden, but there are wonderful fresh fruits and vegetables, unimaginably delicious breads, cakes, and pies, and there's a drink called ambrosia. It tastes like a honey-flavored milkshake but its uniqueness lies in its special ingredient, a pinch of hallucinogen."

"It's got a drug in it?" Mardie was incredulous.

"A *harmless* drug," Mili said, shrugging her shoulders as if to say who should care.

"Are there other drugs in Heaven?"

"Yes."

"Such as?"

"LSD."

"Fuck me!" Mardie's eyes went wide with amazement.

Mili chose to ignore her *and* her expletive. "Aldous Huxley is always using it."

"Aldous Huxley is in Heaven *and* he's using LSD? Where does he get it?"

"I don't know," Mili answered, growing bored with the subject.

"The drug store?"

"Works for me," she told Mili, who tried not to laugh, but did anyway.

Mardie mused over the surprising information about Mr. Brave New World, and added it to Mili's other observations about Heaven. It was a rather quiet and somewhat uneventful place. There weren't many people to be found, and those who were present hadn't much interest in reading or conversing, apparently preferring to smoke, drink, or as in Huxley's case, use drugs. Sounded like the House of Lords.

Pfotenhauer turned his head from the front seat and spoke to Mili.

"We'll be there in just a few minutes, Ms. Wickett."

"Thank you, Pfot."

The scenery outside the car had changed from urban to rural, dry, scruffy countryside, untended and wild. There were vast stretches of brown desert with tumbleweeds rolling across the parched land. It reminded Mardie of the spaghetti westerns she had watched on television as a kid.

"Pfot?" Mili asked. "What was that city we just left?"

"New Babylon, the capital of Hell."

"How perfect," Mili responded, almost purring. "I should have guessed."

Mardie stared at her twin, completely puzzled as to what she was thinking.

"I'm sorry, but I don't understand what you mean."

"New Babylon is named after the most ungodly city in the ancient world," Mili answered, "the capital of the Babylonian Empire." Their armies conquered civilizations across the Fertile Crescent, destroying the Hebrew homeland and enslaving the Jews. Babylon's reputation was so heinous the early Christians called Rome Babylon when its emperors began rounding up and murdering the first European converts."

"But New Babylon doesn't do any of that stuff," Mardie protested.

"That's not the issue. *New* Babylon is an ideal name for the capital of *Hell*. The *worst* city in the *worst* place." Mili looked triumphant.

Chapter Seven

Mardie turned away, humiliated, her arms folded on her chest.

Mili studied her for a moment. "Do you have snail mail down here?"

"Yes, such as it is."

"So your address is New Babylon, Hell, right?"

Mardie nodded, recalling how idiotic she felt when she pasted labels with that on her Christmas cards one year. She shook her head at the memory and giggled.

"What?"

"We exchange Christmas cards here."

Mili looked abashed at Mardie's admission. "Not with Baby Jesus?"

"Of course with Baby Jesus," Mardie answered. "And not just him—angels, wise men, shepherds—everybody!"

Mili howled. "Animals too?" she gasped, glancing at her sister.

"Cows, sheep, donkeys, and camels," Mardie told her.

Mili laughed so hard her sides ached.

Pfot just drove on, shaking his head. Mili had settled down only slightly when she asked Mardie if Santa was also part of Christmas in Hell.

"No, everyone down here is perfectly capable of figuring out who's been naughty."

Mili collapsed again. She only stopped when the BMW began huffing and puffing and losing speed.

Pfot uttered a weary, "Oh no."

"What is it?" Mili asked.

"Another chip set's gone south, I'm afraid. Arrays of integrated circuits control all of the BMW's motor functions. When a chip burns out, the car devolves into a *safe mode,* locking off access to most of the engine's power in an effort to prevent damage to the motor's mechanical components."

"Meaning what exactly?"

"Meaning our speed will keep dropping and our ride will shortly feel somewhat bumpy."

"Does this happen often?"

"Most days."

"Really? Hell must be full of people who can fix this. What about Germans?"

"They designed it."

"Well, I hope they're down here. What about the Swiss?"

"They protect the popes."

"Japanese?"

"There aren't any Japanese in Hell."

Mili snapped her mouth shut. Pfotenhauer struggled to keep the crippled car moving toward Lucifer's estate by pounding the car's gas pedal. The ultimate driving machine lurched drunkenly, trying to satisfy the throttle's demand for power despite the engine's reduced ration of rpm's. It was not a comfortable ride.

"Are we there yet?" Mili asked.

Pfot and Mardie both stared at her, then burst out laughing.

"You did that on purpose," Mardie accused in mock condemnation.

"Suppose I did," Mili shot back in a smart-aleck voice, but then lost her composure and laughed hard. "Pfot, will you turn up the air conditioning, please?" she requested.

"I'm sorry, Ma'am. The AC was deactivated when the chip failed."

Chapter Seven

"That's it," Mili said. "Get Lucifer on the car phone this minute and give him our location. Tell him that I want a new *working* automobile ASAP, and make sure that he knows *I am upset*." Pfot pulled the BMW over and did as he was asked. Everyone put their windows down and waited in the midday heat. Mili took a pen and a pad out of her purse and began writing furiously, filling page after page.

"What are you doing?" Mardie finally got up the nerve to ask.

"I'm listing my conditions of employment," Mili answered, grim faced. "I am not going to put up with cars that break down, nor will I tolerate anything else that doesn't work. I've listed the things I require while I'm working on this case, and every single one of them better function properly, the first time, every time."

"May I read what you wrote?"

"If you wish." Mili flipped back through the pages and pulled out the last page she had written. She handed the pad to Mardie. Mardie read the list from the beginning. It was exhaustive, setting forth Mili's demands in detail: fresh food and wine delivered from *Heaven* for both she and Mardie, along with bottled water, a dispenser capable of chilling it, central air conditioning, all appliances put into good working order, a motorized wheelchair, a ramp at the front of the house, fully functional tools, automobiles, and whatsoever other items she or Mardie required, *plus* new iPhones for her, for Mardie, for Pfotenhauer, *and* for Satan, with adequate reception everywhere in Hell. Mardie admired her sister's pluck. On the other hand, what choice did Lucifer have? If he wanted Mili's services, he'd damn well better come up with everything she asked for. A thin smile crossed Mardie's lips as she envisioned the Devil reading Mili's list. God forbid anything flammable was nearby.

A white Volvo station wagon pulled up next to the disabled Bimmer. While Pfot retrieved the wheelchair and helped Mili out of the car, Mardie studied the blank page beneath the one Mili had removed. Mili pressed her pen hard when she wrote and the page revealed clear impressions of Mili's jottings. Mardie could read them without any difficulty.

> *An iPad with Interpol's fingerprint files downloaded, Any documentation containing information regarding Mardie's damnation. The current whereabouts of likely deceased male, Morgan James Wickett.*

Mardie dropped the pad in her lap and closed her eyes. For the first time in as long as she could remember, she prayed. Oh dear God, no, please.

Chapter Eight

Two giant shapeshifter demons stood at the front gate of Lucifer's compound. At least Mardie hoped they were morphs. The two outsized *cucarachas* brought to life the nightmare creatures she'd dreamed of over and over after she had seen director Scott Ridley's first *Alien* movie. One of these shiny black monsters leaned forward and fixed its gaze on Pfotenhauer.

"'Lo, Pfot," it said. Saliva dripped from its open mouth onto the Volvo door.

"Whoa there, lad," Pfot chided him, and pointed at the glistening spit.

"Oh, sorry," the demon responded and moved back.

"What can I do for you boys?" Pfot asked, quickly wiping up the acid drool with his handkerchief.

"We're to verify that Ms. Wickett is with you." The alien bent its long, almost immovable head down, and looked inside the car.

"Ah, you have *both* Ms. Wicketts. Excellent. Lord Lucifer is not home, but his visitor is still lounging around." The demon barked out a sharp laugh.

"You mean *lying* around, don't you?" the other morph asked.

Both aliens guffawed loudly. One of them managed to bite his tongue and spray acid all over the other's chest.

"Whoa Steve, check this out," the victim exclaimed, staring at the mass of tiny holes being etched all across his black shell. In moments the shell began to sag and looked on the brink of total dissolution. Then the acid stopped.

"Far out, Butch!" the morph uttered in awe, then pointed a handheld device at the gate and stepped aside as it opened. Mardie watched the two demons as Pfotenhauer drove through. They transformed into crimson-colored humanoid shapes as Steve quickly checked Butch's chest to see if any of the acid had eaten into his real skin. She hoped it had, was Mardie's reaction, and she hoped it hurt. Morons.

Mardie got her first glance at Lucifer's house. It was a rambling two-story spec home from the 1920s, or maybe the 1930s, painted white with brown trim and a porch.

"Lucifer lives *here*?" she asked, almost sure there must be some mistake.

"He does," Pfot answered her. "His home is rather humble. He had it modeled on the one owned by Chicago mayor Richard J. Daley who, despite his absolute control of the lives of Chicagoans, resided in a modest home right up to the day he died. Mr. Daley told the Master that if a person wielded real power, there was no need to advertise it by living in a castle."

Pfotenhauer pulled the car up to the front door. A short, orange demon hustled out of the house, carefully avoiding the all-too-visible corpse lying on the steps. When Pfot raised the trunk, the little devil reached in for the wheelchair, opened it, and placed it beside Mili's car door. He offered his hand as Mili stepped out and carefully helped her into the chair.

Chapter Eight

"Why are you orange?" she asked.

"Because I'm Protestant," he replied.

Mili laughed.

"There are green ones, too," the demon added, as though making a case for his color.

"I'd be heartbroken if there weren't," Mili replied, and patted the demon on the shoulder.

Mardie got out of the car and walked around the back of the Volvo. She was immediately hit by the smell, a pungent, sour rot that permeated the air. She forced herself to stand next to Mili, who was already studying the body. The dead man lay sprawled on his chest, swollen and bloated, a thick brown sludge congealed around his body. Suddenly Mardie felt lightheaded. Then nauseated. She knew she was going to have to vomit. She clasped her mouth with her hand and turned away. She felt bile in her throat, but refused to yield to the terror of the smell of violent death. After a long moment, she looked at the corpse again. Her eyes were drawn to the raw flesh where the victim's head had been wrenched away. The skin was a mottled gray with smears of dried blood caked around the torn edges.

"I don't see any maggots," Mili said, surprise in her voice, "nor evidence of larger scavengers." She looked at Mardie. "Are there any wild animals in Hell?"

"Only human ones."

Mili gave Mardie an amused look, then looked at Pfotenhauer.

"I'm sorry to ask, dear boy, but would you mind turning the body over for me?"

With nary a word of protest, Pfot bent down, lifted one side of the corpse, and rolled it onto its back.

"Oh my God," Mardie gasped. Mili simply stared. The man's shirt was ripped open, exposing a large cavity where his organs had once been. Mili leaned forward in her wheelchair and studied the hole. It was mushy and messy, with shreds of flesh, vessels, and veins clinging to the crater inside the rib cage.

Mili sat back up. "Your description was deucedly accurate," she said to Mardie. "Congratulations. The victim was indeed killed and gutted elsewhere, then brought here and beheaded. But why? And where's the head?"

Mardie didn't know, and head or no head, she'd seen enough of the wretched human casualty and walked away. She gazed at Lucifer's house. It looked sad and nondescript. The King of Hell lived in a dump. Mayor Daley must have been one powerful son of a bitch to own a place like that. She had no doubt that Satan was as well.

"Mardie?" Mili called. Mardie turned back, pinching her nose against the stink. "Pfot is going to drive us to your house now, if that's all right with you. I've got him calling Lucifer to get the body moved to some kind of refrigerated storage. As soon as he's done, we're gone.

Mardie nodded, then noticed something by the body. "Have you seen that already?" she asked Mili, pointing her finger at a swath of blood that led away from the corpse. She walked along the smear to where it ended at the edge of the tarmac. She looked back at Mili. "It finishes here."

Mili pushed her chair down the driveway to where Mardie was standing. "Actually, the smear *begins* here," she corrected her sister, studying the dried swirl of blood. "The body must have originally lain on this spot, only to be dragged up onto Satan's steps. How curious." She looked at Mardie. Her face was flushed and her eyes were shining.

"How *fun*, you mean," Mardie said, intending to be caustic. It was obvious that Mili's involvement in Hell's first murder had gotten her very excited.

Chapter Eight

Her twin stared at her for a moment, then narrowed her eyes and grinned a wicked grin.

"I'm glad you think so," she whispered. "Me, too!"

✳ ✳ ✳

The twins were at the kitchen table having tea. Mardie had settled Mili into her own bedroom, lovingly decorated with a French Empire four-poster bed, a creamy white dresser with golden highlights and a matching armoire, a pink-and-champagne striped love seat, and a set of mauve drapes on the windows.

Mili appreciated Mardie's kindness in giving up her bedroom, but failed to comment on anything other than a small walnut desk and chair, which she immediately adopted as her "work station." Mardie was not offended. She had already learned that her sister possessed a rather narrow set of interests, working and eating, or talking about working and eating.

For afternoon tea, Mardie had brewed up some Twinings she'd bought on a street corner from a demon who'd boasted he'd brought it all the way from London's Fleet Street. His Berlitz British accent made her suspicious, but after one whiff of the bags in the box, she handed over what he asked. She poured tea for Mili, and set cream and sugar next to her cup, along with a white linen napkin and a silver teaspoon. She also set out a crystal bowl filled with sugared walnuts. Mili proceeded to scoop them up by the handful, and Mardie actually had to refill the bowl before she could sit down.

"How extensively do you use internet down here?" Mili asked, pouring a generous amount of cream into her tea, followed by multiple spoons of white sugar. Mardie tried not to count, but couldn't stop herself. Six.

"I don't use the internet," she said.

"Well, actually you do, though you may not be aware of it. You have a computer with a web camera attached, and you now have a mobile phone, both of which connect to the internet using a service provider or Wi-Fi."

"Why did you ask me if you already knew?"

"What I actually was wondering was *how* you use internet," Mili clarified. "News? Entertainment? Email? I mean, where else could you go for such things?"

"We don't have any of those things."

"Where do you go when you have a question?"

"The phone operator. She connects me to someone who can help."

Mili arched an eyebrow. "That's a bit old-fashioned." She pronounced old-fashioned as though she were describing a pastry with a spoiled filling. "How did you get on when you first arrived here? Pay phones?"

"Very funny," Mardie said. "I have to admit, though, that the transition was a bit odd. One moment I was lying in a hospital bed fighting to take one last breath, and the next I was standing in a queue, part of a line shuffling toward two fire-red demons standing behind podiums just like security officials at Heathrow. When my turn came I was given temporary lodging, coupons for food, and printed sheets listing jobs and places to live. No one specifically told me that I was in Hell, but gazing at the red chaps with horns was a pretty good clue. Then I saw the stark buildings, the almost nonexistent traffic, and the total absence of trees and flowers. I tried to fool myself into thinking I might be in one of those broken down post-Communist 'Stans, Kazakhstan, Kyrgyzstan, Uzbekistan, yadda, yadda, yadda, but I finally had to admit that I couldn't be any other place *except* Hell."

Chapter Eight

"I see," Mili said.

Mardie looked at her. Mili's facial expression was neutral, just like her words. *I see.* It reminded her of every other cop she'd ever dealt with. Reasonable at first. Then the cuffs came out. Mardie wondered what had happened to Mili when she had arrived in Heaven. She suspected it had been a bit more welcoming than Hell. Luncheon for the newly sainted? Tutorials on how to get the most out of your eternal life? Angels for mentors and good deed doers for friends?

"I woke up in Heaven after I died," Mili shared, apparently reading Mardie's mind. "I found myself resting on the most comfortable bed I had ever been on, in a lovely bedroom done in bright Caribbean island colors and white wicker furniture. There were picture windows with cloudless skies and gently rolling meadows stretching as far as I could see. I was told later that day that I was at a hotel designated for new arrivals. Over the next few days, there were introductory sessions to life in Heaven and angels standing by to answer questions. It all felt rather like that chipper little American movie, you know, the one with Albert Brooks and Meryl Streep."

Mardie remembered that flick all too well, but chipper was not a word she would have used to describe the very painful ninety minutes of cinema she had experienced. Meryl's and Albert's characters meet at a facility somewhere beyond the Earth for persons who have just died. The post-death process involves several rounds of formal interviews with Heaven's bureaucrats aimed at determining whether the newly deceased will be allowed to move on to a higher life-form or return to Earth for reincarnation. Mardie found the movie terribly hard to watch, witnessing the protagonist's weaknesses highlighted, his squandered opportunities disclosed, and worst of all, his debilitating fears examined in minute detail, every one of his failures played out in videos from his life. Chipper? Really.

The Wickett Sisters in Hell

"So do you like Heaven?" Mardie asked Mili.

"To be honest, I haven't made any friends, and, obviously, there is no work for *me* to do. I'd have to say, God forgive me, that Heaven is rather boring. You can't imagine how cheered up I was when I found out that Lucifer had requested my help."

"Who told you? Jehovah?"

"Oh no," Mili replied, shaking her head. "The Archangel Gabriel did, which was still quite an honor. He discussed the particulars, explaining that God was hopeful that I would see my way clear to lending a hand."

"Did you think it strange that He was willing to help the Devil?"

"I never gave it a moment's thought. All I knew was that I was being offered a case." Mili's eyes glittered. "An extraordinary case. I mean, a murder in Hell? Who'd ever heard of such a thing?"

"Did anyone tell you that you'd be staying with me?"

"Yes, Gabriel did. I have to admit I was a bit concerned, not having seen you for such a long time. But I hoped for the best, and here I am."

"And here you are," Mardie echoed. Mili's comments about staying with her weren't much of an endorsement.

Mili drank the last of her tea. "Can you come with me for a moment?" she asked Mardie, then backed her wheelchair away from the table and led her to the desk in the bedroom. She picked up her new iPad.

"Have you ever seen one of these?" She held up the sleek device.

Mardie shook her head. "But I would guess it's some kind of portable computer. I used terminals hooked up to mainframes at work, but I saw people typing away on the likes of those at Starbucks. Here at home I just use paper and a pen."

"How endearing. You are so traditional."

Chapter Eight

"So out of it is what you really mean."

Mili turned the iPad on. "I want to see if Interpol downloaded the fingerprint files I requested."

"It sounds like you're already into the case."

"Quite so. In fact, Pfotenhauer is stopping by later to take me to see the murder victim again. Do you want to go along?"

Mardie's stomach instantly seized up at the mere mention of the grotesquely mutilated body. "Why would you go back again?" she managed to ask.

"I need to perform some standard homicide procedures," Mili answered, fiddling with the iPad.

"Such as?"

"Examining wounds, determining which were superficial and which were fatal. Also, scanning for odd things like unusual marks or stains, and then wrapping it up by taking photographs." Mili looked up from the iPad. "Now that doesn't sound so terrible, does it?" Her face took on a winsome, inviting expression. "Come along. I promise not to gross you out."

Before Mardie could answer, Mili's iPad beeped. She read a message on her monitor. "Well, Hell," she said, disgusted. "The files haven't been sent yet." Mili frowned, then pressed various buttons until another file opened up. She grinned, cried *yes*, and waved her iPad in the air. "But my game is here!" she exclaimed, happily. "Hangman. Ha!"

Chapter Nine

MILI TOOK THE IPAD BACK TO THE KITCHEN TABLE and played hangman while Mardie put the kettle on for another round of tea.

"Are there any more of those scrumptious walnuts?" Mili asked.

"No, but I have some chocolates." Mardie hated to keep shoveling sugary things toward her sister, but she told herself that Mili was safe now from the disease that had ravaged her.

"Oh yes, please," Mili entreated, talking while tapping icons on her iPad screen. Mardie took the crystal bowl and filled it with the Godiva truffles that had arrived from Heaven. Someone up there knew Mili. She set the chocolates by her sister, then sat down at the table and watched as she unwrapped chocolate after chocolate without missing a move on her game.

"Isaac Asimov," Mili said, after a while.

"The writer?"

"Yes."

"What about him?"

"I was thinking of people I'd seen in Heaven that you might recognize."

"Isaac Asimov, the *atheist*, is in Heaven?"

Chapter Nine

"One and the same," Mili replied, eyes fixed on her game.

"And you saw him?"

"Yes. He was having coffee with Kurt Vonnegut."

"Kurt Vonnegut is in Heaven, too?" Mardie couldn't believe what she was hearing.

"He wouldn't have been sitting there with his coffee and his cigarettes if he wasn't."

"Well, not every unbeliever is up there," she retorted, angry at what she was hearing. "I see plenty of them down here every day."

"This isn't a contest," Mili insisted.

"Oh yes, it is. Collective us versus collective you."

"Don't be absurd."

"Say what you will," Mardie snapped, and in a moment announced, "Chaucer."

"Please don't."

"Richard the Lionheart."

"Well, that's no surprise."

"Margaret Thatcher."

"Ditto, and I'm glad to hear it."

"Princess Diana."

"No!" Mili stared at Mardie, horrified.

Mardie nodded and got up to make the tea. It was the best she'd felt since Mili had arrived.

✳✳✳

The bloated mass that had once been a man lay face up on a butcher's steel table. Flayed cattle carcasses hoisted up on hooks and chains hung behind him. Satan's minions had located a blackmarket slaughterhouse willing to store the cadaver.

The Wickett Sisters in Hell

"Gases are venting through the abdominal cavity," Mili said, pointing at the cadaver's scraped out ribcage, "otherwise he'd be even more bloated." She studied the man's gutted torso.

"This chap is missing a lot of his stuffing, isn't he?"

Mardie stared at the cadaver. Everything from the individual's throat down to his pelvis was absent. Just absolutely gone. She looked at Mili. "Winston Churchill," she said.

Mili stared at her a moment, trying to process her random comment. "Excuse me?"

"Just remembered he's down here, too."

"Don't be childish." She looked back at the corpse. "D. H. Lawrence is in Heaven."

"Wuss. You can have him."

Mili stretched a finger toward the corpse.

"Oh, please don't touch that with your bare finger," Mardie said quickly. "It's full of dangerous germs."

"Nonsense. That's nothing but an old wives' tale. Unless a person expires from a contagious disease, his or her corpse poses no threat to the living."

"I still don't want you to touch it."

Mili rolled her eyes. "Did you understand what I just told you?"

"I did. Don't touch it."

"*Fine.* I'll wear some gloves. See if there are any disposables around here."

Mardie found precisely what Mili wanted, a box of latex gloves sitting on top of a beat-up metal desk, along with a red plastic bucket full of knives, a roll of paper towels, a police-style service revolver splattered with dried blood, and a framed five-by-seven color photograph. She leaned down and looked at the picture. It looked like

Chapter Nine

it had been taken at some holiday party, the slaughterhouse crew of green demons posing merrily for the camera. Well, crikey. The orange demon had been telling the truth.

Mardie yanked a pair of gloves out of the box and took them to Mili. Her sister pulled them on and lifted one of the man's hands, carefully examining its palm. She grimaced and swore, "Christ Almighty."

"Hey!" Mardie protested.

Mili glanced at her. "What? You curse down here. I've heard you."

"Not like that, I don't. I'd think people from Heaven would be more respectful."

"Yes? Well, we're not in Heaven, are we? We're in Hell, examining a local who somehow managed to get himself offed. This is neither the place nor the situation where I feel obliged to watch my language."

Mardie shook her head, but held her tongue. Mili turned her attention to the fingers of the hand she was holding, then dropped it. It went *thud* against the metal table.

Mardie cringed.

"Sorry," Mili said. "Bad habit." She checked the cadaver's other hand and put it back down. "The killer cut off this man's fingerprints and skinned his palms."

Mardie's stomach rumbled. She quickly put a hand up to her mouth.

"Not here," Mili warned. Mardie nodded, and after a moment put her hand back down. "It appears that the murderer went to extremes to make sure his victim was not easily identifiable. No face, no prints. I don't suppose you have DNA labs here?"

"For what purpose?"

"Paternity suits."

Mardie just stared at her twin.

"I'm kidding. There probably isn't one in Heaven, either. Maybe I can get a loaner from Scotland Yard."

"I'd love to see their faces when they get your request."

"It would take some careful wording, eh? Dear former colleagues. This is Mili Wickett in Hell. Heh, heh," she chuckled. "Actually, this is the sort of thing Lucifer should be able to handle. My guess is that he's pretty well-connected on Earth."

"You're going to try to perform a DNA identification on this corpse?"

"Why not? As I told you, everybody in Hell has been reconstructed based on the genomes of their own DNA, so it's only a matter of referencing this cadaver's genetic material against the data in Lucifer's resident files."

"Why not just ask God who it is?"

Mili shook her head. "He's not going to make anything easy for the Devil."

"But He sent you."

"That doesn't mean He's going to solve the Devil's problems."

"Have you ever seen Jehovah?" Mardie asked.

"No, and neither have most folks. How many Brits have ever seen the Queen? Ratchet that up two or three magnitudes and you have the odds of running into God in Paradise."

Mili's eye was drawn to a discolored spot on one of the corpse's arms. She rubbed the area then looked for other such marks. She found more on his arms and legs.

"Nicotine residue. Wherever the killer handled the body he left these discolorations on the skin. Takes a very heavy smoker to do that. His fingertips were probably the color of a flower stamen."

Chapter Nine

Mili's mobile phone rang inside her purse.

"Be a dear and grab it, will you?"

Mardie reached in her sister's purse and pulled out the phone. Satan's face was on the miniature screen.

"It's Lucifer," she said, and turned the phone toward Mili.

"Press the *On* button."

Mardie did so.

"Hello?"

"Where are you?" Satan asked, agitated.

"At the temporary morgue where the body was moved."

"Well, sorry to interrupt you, but I thought you should know that another body just showed up."

"My God." Mili was stunned.

"I'm standing on my front steps looking at it."

"Is it mutilated like the last one?"

"No, this one still has its head. And its face. The rest of the body has been scorched black, right down to the toes."

"I'm not going," Mardie said after the call.

"It won't be as bad as you imagine," her sister replied.

"It's already worse than *this* one." Mardie pointed at the headless body.

"I could use the extra pair of eyes," Mili said. "You were the one who saw the smear of blood. Who knows what you'll see this time."

"A big blistered corpse from what I just heard."

"There will be more to see than that; there always is. Do please come."

Mardie did. She had promised Lucifer after all. It was almost dusk by the time they arrived at Satan's estate. Pfotenhauer slowed as he approached the closed security gates.

"Does it get dark here at night?" Mili asked, looking at the sky.

"Yes. This isn't Alaska where the sun shines at midnight."

"I was thinking of Heaven. It's bright during the day, and seems to never get totally dark at night."

"It turns black here. And there aren't any streetlights."

"Is it dangerous?"

"Don't know. Never went out at night until you showed up."

The security gates swung open as Pfotenhauer approached. He gave a friendly wave to the pair of twelve-foot Tyrannosaurus Rex as he drove in. Mardie stared at the dinosaurs, who stared back. She was sure they had to be the same goof-off demons who'd passed themselves off as xenomorphs the first time she'd been here. Now they were dinosaurs. Maybe with a little luck they'd turn themselves in black holes.

Pfot pulled the car right up to Lucifer's front door. He helped Mili into her wheelchair while Mardie waited inside the car. She was determined not to be the first person to view the burned man, who, as it turned out, was stretched out on the tarmac right next to her side of the car. She would have put her foot right on him if Pfotenhauer hadn't warned her when he opened her door. She stepped over the blackened corpse, looking at it just long enough to make sure she didn't brush it with her shoe. Mili, on the other hand, nudged her wheelchair right up to the body. She cocked her head, as if trying to take everything in all at once. The victim was male, tall and heavyset, with ferocious black burns covering his body, like a wiener that had been dropped into the campfire.

"Oh dear," Mili muttered as she studied the terrible burns. "What do you suppose happened here?" She ran her eyes up and down the cadaver. "Ankles and wrists were tied. The body was bound upright, across the chest, maybe to a chair. The hair is partly singed

Chapter Nine

away, but the face is undamaged. These injuries resemble the kind of thing a blowtorch could do. I don't see evidence of cuts, punctures, blows, or bullet wounds, though they may well be concealed by the burns."

"His throat is burned away," Mardie said. "I wonder if he suffocated to death."

"Splendid observation," Mili told her. "Note that the victim's face is contorted and his mouth agape, as if he was gasping for air at the end. Poor bastard likely suffocated to death."

Mili reached down and lifted one of the victim's hands. The palm and fingers were blistered and raw. Burned clean away. Mardie hoped the man had been dead first. No prints again. Yet the face had been left alone. Why?

"Jesus, Joseph, and Mary," a voice said. Mili and Mardie looked up to see Lucifer standing at the top of the steps. "Have you ever seen anything like that?" The Devil was frowning, but he didn't look away. "Why do you suppose the killer spared the victim's face?"

"We were just wondering the same thing," Mili answered. "He burned off the corpse's palm and finger prints. Yet he left the face alone. It might well be a provocation after the success of his first kill."

"You think it's the same murderer?"

"Based on where we found both bodies, the likely answer is yes, and you, without a doubt, are the target of his grotesqueries." Mili paused a moment to let that sink in, and then went on. "I do not know whether the murderer is from Earth or Hell, and I am unable to say whether his victims are from either. But whoever the killer is, he can apparently march right in and dump his victims at your door. Until we know more about who he is, and what his intentions are, we have to consider that he may only be toying with these murders as a prelude to trying to kill you."

Lucifer grimaced, his face suddenly lined and weary. "No one's ever tried that before, and I certainly don't understand what the point would be to try now. If there ever was an overrated power in this Universe, it would be me."

"I think that's a bit modest," Mili reacted. "Many people on Earth live in fear of your plans and intentions, and hundreds of millions of Christians, Jews, and Muslims believe that you are the source of all manner of evil. I would suggest that you take precautions."

The ruler of Hell looked silently at the tortured corpse. Mili wondered if indeed Lucifer could be wounded and murdered as this man had been. Or was he invulnerable, immortal? Whatever the case, he might very soon be fighting off someone intent on killing him.

Lucifer gazed at Mili.

"I will heed your advice. I am not going to cower, however. This person thinks that I can't find him. Let's start by proving him wrong." Lucifer turned to Pfotenhauer. "Pfot, track down Robert Capa and get him over here. I want photographs of the victim's face and I want them delivered to my office tonight."

Lucifer addressed Mili again. "Call me with anything you discover about either of the two victims." His voice trailed off, anger suddenly contorting his handsome face. "*Two* victims. I can't believe I'm saying that. *Two* victims in *two* days."

Small flickers of flame popped up on the top of Lucifer's head.

Mili stared in wonder. Both Mardie and Pfotenhauer stepped back as fast as they could.

Chapter Ten

"The Devil is not at all like I envisioned," Mili observed after Lucifer had stalked back into his house.

"And yet, he sort of is," Mardie said.

"Yes, sort of." She thought of the various moods she'd seen Satan demonstrate during her short time in Hell. "What's with the pyrotechnics?"

"I've only seen it one other time. It appears to happen when he gets very upset."

"Good to know."

Both sisters reflected on Lucifer's temper for a moment. It was much more disturbing than either of them cared to admit.

Mili looked at Mardie. "I apologize if this seems extraordinarily out of place, I mean with a dead man lying here and all, but I really need a candy bar."

"There's nothing around here, I'm afraid. Why don't I have Pfot take me home while you do what you need to do here? By the time you catch up with me I'll have dinner *and* dessert ready."

Mili looked pleased. "May I have extra dessert?"

"Easy peasy," Mardie replied. She and her twin froze. Mardie had inadvertently used one of their mother's favorite phrases, one she had cheerfully used when Mili asked for sweets. The awkward moment passed, but it unsettled Mardie so much she blurted out her unhappiness over another issue that had been festering ever since Mili had arrived.

"Why didn't you tell me when Mom died?" she asked.

Mili looked at her, her face stiff and defensive. "Why would you have wanted to know?"

"She was my mother."

"You never acted like her daughter."

"Because I didn't make a pact of death with her like you did?"

Mili's face crumpled. She didn't defend herself against Mardie's accusation. Its obvious truth was devastating. Instead, she responded with an apology cloaked as penance.

"Maybe we should just skip dessert tonight?"

Mardie felt her heart sink. She'd expected a vicious row over her mother's favoritism toward Mili. Instead her sister refused to fight back, and in the only way a sugar addict could apparently atone for her sin, she was offering to punish herself by giving up her dessert. As broken and pathetic as that was, Mardie couldn't help but feel bad for her twin.

"No need," Mardie responded. "I was wrong to bring that up now. You've got enough to carry without me trying to break your back with my issues."

"No," Mili replied. "I need to hear how you feel. I thought you hated Mother, or I would have called you." Mili stopped and shook her head. "No, that's just another excuse. She was your mum. I should have called you, period."

"I am going to make chocolate mousse," Mardie said. "Would you like it with whipped cream and slivered almonds?"

"That sounds wonderful," Mili answered. "Does this mean you forgive me?"

Chapter Ten

"No. In that case, I would have added brandied cherries."

Mili smiled.

Pfotenhauer walked up.

"Did you find Capa?" Mili asked.

"Yes. He's on his way, but he's going to stop and pick up some floodlights."

"All right. I've got some work to do on the body, but I want you to run Mardie home."

Mardie started toward the car but turned to ask Mili a last question.

"Do you really think someone might try to kill Lucifer?"

"I do. Imagine a person down here who wants revenge because he or she believes that he ruined their Earthly life or even tempted them to commit the sins that led to their damnation. Further imagine that such an individual possesses a history of violence, was even perhaps a murderer in his mortal life, and is now framing his revenge in the only terms he understands: homicide. Whatever our killer's intent may be, he has singled out Lucifer, baiting him by dropping dead bodies on his personal turf, yet making it almost impossible for him to discover who they are, let alone who he is.

"At some point the taunting will likely evolve into something even more personal, blowing up Satan's car, burning down his house, killing his staff or driver. Such actions would not only be hurtful, but might also be tests of Lucifer's vulnerability, leading finally and, I believe, inexorably, to an attack on the Devil himself."

"If I were Lucifer, I'd start worrying," Mardie said.

Both she and Mili thought about that for a moment, then Mardie walked on toward the car with Pfotenhauer behind her.

By the time he dropped Mardie at the house and returned, Robert Capa was taking shots of the body. Pfot told him hello, and asked Mili if she was ready to leave. She was.

On the way Pfot asked her how it had gone with Capa. Mili told him that the war photographer was upset about recent allegations maligning one of his most famous photos from the Spanish Civil War. She, in turn, had told him that the photographs he was taking now might well bear witness to the beginning of an even more shocking conflict.

Pfot asked how Capa took that.

"He gave me his business card and told me to call him if somebody else turned up dead."

Mili sat at the kitchen table holding a crystal snifter filled with green-colored absinthe, a half dozen sugar cubes dissolving at the bottom. She and Mardie were chatting while Mardie set the table and completed the dinner preparations. She had made artichoke soup, Caesar salad, veal piccata, boiled red potatoes, and green beans. Three chocolate mousse desserts were chilling in the icebox. Two of them were for Mili.

"It's so nice that you cook," Mili said as Mardie set linen napkins and silver tableware. "Who taught you?"

"Loneliness." She reached for her wine glass and took a sip of Merlot. "Actually, I watch a lot of cooking folks on the telly."

"Culinary legends, every one."

"More like quiz show hosts. Better at being charming than cooking."

"I love the one with six-inch heels and born-again cleavage."

Chapter Ten

"You've heard of that crazy woman?"

"Worse. I've watched her. I must confess she made the most sinfully delicious cupcakes I've ever seen."

"Then it's only a matter of time until she's down here with us."

Mili giggled.

Mardie topped off her absinthe and dropped in four more sugar cubes.

"Speaking of chefs, you know that we have Julia Child in Heaven, right?" Mili asked.

Mardie snorted with derision.

"Pardon me?"

"Any *real* French chef, and every one who ever won a Michelin star, is down here."

"Touché."

"Might as well give it up, sis. You can't win."

"You may have chefs, but you also have every kidnapper, every bank robber, every rapist, and every serial killer who ever lived."

"Sore loser. I'm just surprised you haven't asked to meet the ones who managed to slip through the hands of the law."

"What on Earth is that supposed to mean?"

"Simply that you have a unique opportunity to parlay with the very criminals who—" Mardie paused, then whispered dramatically, "—escaped!"

"Good Heavens. You're absolutely right. What made you think of that?"

"After our earlier talk about a killer on Earth becoming a killer in Hell, I began wondering whether perhaps one of those infamous psychopathic ne'er-do-wells had indeed figured out how to indulge in his former habits down here again."

Mili set her glass down and stared at Mardie. "Sweet Jesus.

Can you imagine? Never caught on Earth and now roaming loose in Hell?"

Mardie shuddered and reached for her wine. There was a knock at the front door. She locked eyes with Mili, both of them unnerved at the unexpected arrival. Mardie wiped her hands on a towel and headed to the door. She looked out the peephole. It was Pfotenhauer. He waved at her. You're not supposed to know I'm looking at you, she thought, and opened the door.

"Pfot, don't take this wrong, but I'm sort of surprised to see you again tonight."

Pfotenhauer smiled coyly and waved a manila envelope. "I asked Capa to make copies for Miss Mili."

"Oh, Pfot," Mardie said, instantly regretting her comment. "How thoughtful of you. We were just sitting down to dinner. Why don't you join us?"

Pfotenhauer stood without moving.

"I cooked chicken piccata."

Pfotenhauer still didn't move. "I've never been invited to someone's home before," he finally said.

Mardie felt her heart tug. "Oh, Pfot. We would be happy to have you join us."

"Thank you, I accept," he said shyly. "Now I know what folks mean when they said they'd died and gone to Heaven."

Mardie choked up, then stepped aside so Pfot could come in.

Chapter Eleven

"W E'VE GOT TO STOP MEETING THIS WAY," Mili said. "Otherwise you'll be as fat as me."

"Ha!" Mardie laughed, frying bacon and eggs on the iron stove. Mili was at the table drinking her first tea of the day, while Mardie fixed breakfast for them both. "So how did you sleep on that big bed?" she asked.

"Wonderfully well, thank you," Mili said, adding cream to her tea. "And my, is it big! Is there some naughty reason why you bought one so large?"

"Thank you for that, but it's a copy of the great bed at the Victoria and Albert Museum. Used to run in there for a peek during lunch hour whenever I could."

"Are you talking about the famous old bed mentioned in Shakespeare's Twelfth Night?"

"The very same. Sleeps sixteen. Well, *holds* sixteen anyway."

Mili grinned and added sugar to her tea. Mardie watched out of the corner of her eye how many spoons she took. Six. Egad.

"Do you still have diabetes?" she asked.

Mili frowned and a distinct sourness appeared in her tone.

"Delicately asked, and no, I don't. There are no diseases in Heaven."

Mardie turned from the stove and looked at her sister. "Then why is one of your feet missing?"

Mili's face drooped. She didn't break eye contact though, and answered honestly.

"You are asking a very personal question, and regretfully, it is one that I cannot answer. When I woke in Heaven, I saw that I was still a cripple. I was told that some people in Heaven continue to be marked by the infirmities they carried on Earth and that I was one."

"What kind of eternal crap is that? Did you ask for more information?"

"Of course I did, and I always got the same answer. I had been saved, but I had not been made whole."

"That's bloody nonsense," Mardie spat out. She knew her kvetching wasn't going to make Mili feel any better, but it really did seem incredibly cold of Jehovah to make a new Heavenly body for Mili with her old infirmity. Truth was, it wasn't just cold, it was cruel.

Mardie filled Mili's teacup, as well as the cream and sugar. She could tell Mili was miffed at her for asking about her condition, but everlasting life with one foot unaccounted for? Brilliant. On the other hand she was facing her own immortal existence with wrinkles, aches and pains, and white hair she had to dye the living shit out of to get blond. Made her wonder, not for the first time, whether God got off on all this. Not her place to bitch about it? She was in Hell. She had a right to bitch about anything she wanted.

Mardie served the bacon and eggs and brought toast in a clever little slice holder that carried four pieces ready to butter. Able to build the world's greatest empire and still find time to invent the ultimate toast server? Only the British. The Wickett sisters ate in

Chapter Eleven

silence, each being tugged at by their own private thoughts, when the phone rang. Mili reached for the receiver and Pfotenhauer's face appeared on the monitor.

"Well, good morning, Pfot. What's the news?"

"Good morning, Miss Mili. Lucifer is requesting that you and Miss Mardie come to his office and examine a batch of photographs he's pulled from Hell's archives."

"Photographs of whom?"

"Residents who resemble the man in the pictures taken by Mr. Capa last evening."

"All right."

"Would a pickup half an hour from now be suitable?"

"Eminently suitable."

"Thank you, then. May I also speak to Miss Mardie for a moment?"

"Of course."

Mili held out the receiver to her twin.

"Yes?" Mardie asked, looking at Pfotenhauer on the screen.

"I just wanted to say thank you again for dinner last night, Miss Mardie." The diminutive chauffeur spoke with great earnestness. "I will remember it forever."

"Pfot, it was our pleasure to have you, believe me."

"I may have drank a bit too much of your wine, though, Miss," he continued apologetically. "Did I get carried away with my stories?"

"Not a bit, Pfot. Tales of notable murders and singular dismemberments performed by the London mob had a perfect place in the evening's discussions of unidentified corpses and whatnot. You were a delightful guest. Truly. We'll do it again, I promise."

"Thank you, Miss Mardie." Pfot saluted.

The Wickett Sisters in Hell

"You're so welcome. Goodbye." Mardie replaced the receiver on its hook.

"So, will you accompany me to view the photographs the Devil has found? I just read an email from him. He says there are three possible matches."

"Three? Is that good?"

"Who knows? Come with me and we'll find out together."

"All right, if you want me to."

"I do," Mili assured her. "How a resident could even be killed down here is way beyond where I'm at in this investigation, and it nags at me. Having you close somehow helps me persevere."

Mardie looked at her sister. Her sister did not speak again, but she treasured what she had said and stored it away in her heart.

Lucifer sat at his desk surrounded by Wicketts and clerks. He was wearing a golden robe that matched the color of his curls, its neck and cuffs highlighted with royal blue piping. Mili thought he looked just like an angel. Mardie was pretty sure she'd seen someone wearing the same costume on a gay pride parade float. Either way, the Lord of Hell was clearly steamed up by the two back-to-back homicides.

He had laid several large black-and-white photographs on his desk. One of them was a Capa close-up of the burned man's unburned face. The rest were file photographs of Hell's residents.

"Have a look, and tell me if you think that one of these photos matches the face of the burned victim," Lucifer asked Mili. His request was polite enough, but his voice was tense and irritable. Everyone in the room cringed at his raw tone and covertly looked to see if flames had erupted on his head or shoulders. Mili had not yet observed what

Chapter Eleven

happened when Lucifer's temper flared, but she remembered the odd little tongues of flame that had appeared on his head last night when he became upset. She also noted with a thrill of dread that all of the furniture in the Devil's office was made of asbestos.

She pulled the photographs toward herself and studied them carefully. When she finished Mili looked up at Lucifer, who was watching her with undisguised impatience. If the Devil thought his first cut at identifying the burn victim had been successful, he was about to be disappointed. "There is no doubt that your computer has isolated images of several people down here who indeed seem to closely resemble the dead man's face," Mili began. "If we were interested in speed versus justice, we could just pick any one of these possibilities and think we had identified the dead man. But the fact that all the photographs appear to match the corpse's face simply underscores the fact that an apparent similarity between a picture and the face of the cadaver is not enough to positively identify this victim. Something more tangible is required." Mili saw the flickering of tiny fires erupt across the top of Lucifer's head. It was alarming, but she steeled herself and forged on. "On Earth, a victim sans fingerprints may still be identified using professional dental records, or medical files documenting physical abnormalities, surgical interventions, chronic diseases, broken bones, et cetera, et cetera. Do such records exist down here that would allow us to match charts and cadavers as it were?"

"Hellions," Satan corrected her. The Devil was not pleased at being told his photos were being dismissed, but for all that, his little flames of discontent slowly faded away. Mili frowned, not recognizing Lucifer's term. "Bodies created for the damned are called Hellions."

"Hellions?" she repeated.

Lucifer nodded.

"Hellions," Mili repeated again. "All right. Now back to my question. Do records exist in Hell that could be used to confirm the identity of the deceased?"

Satan did not speak. No one spoke. Mili decided to try a different tact.

"If we cannot produce records to prove the identity of the victim, does a pathology exist whereby we can at least prove that the cadaver, both cadavers actually, are, in fact, Hellions? We could then at least eliminate the possibility that either body may have been transported here from Earth." Mili addressed the question to everyone, but she and Lucifer knew whom she was speaking to. "And please, don't tell me that the corpses can't be brought here from Earth," she went on, focusing her eyes on Satan. "I've been here long enough already to know that if *you* can get anything you want delivered down here, it is very likely that some of your more nefarious demons are able to bring a body down here as well."

Lucifer's face turned red, flames erupted on his head and shoulders and raced down his sleeves. Mardie pushed her chair back, as did everyone else seated around the desk. Only Mili sat still and stared at the furious Devil.

"Temper, temper," she said.

Fire exploded from Lucifer's body and the heat blasted everyone. Flames jumped off his body and landed on the tabletop. Mili slammed them out with her palm and scowled at Lucifer.

He, however, was no longer physically recognizable, having condensed into a blazing, white-hot fireball blazing away in the chair. The heat was so intense that even Mili had to finally push her wheelchair back. Then she locked down the wheels, held her ground, and shouted at Lucifer, "Let me do my job, or I quit!"

Chapter Eleven

In an instant the fire was gone and Lucifer reappeared again on his chair, sitting upright, pale as a corpse. His eyes were gun-barrel blue and hard as steel. His words, however, were conciliatory and calm.

"I'd rather you didn't do that," he said. It wasn't an apology, but it was an admission, and that was good enough for Mili. She unlocked the wheels on her chair and moved back to the desk.

Lucifer looked at her with grudging admiration, albeit with undisguised resentment.

"We have never had this issue before, but I would think that a basic yet reliable method of distinguishing an Earthly body from a Hellion body would be the condition of the internal tissues. While Hellion citizens still show the outward wear and tear that wore their mortal bodies down, their internal systems, blood, bile, nerves, and organs are revitalized. In a word, immortal."

"I beg your pardon, sir," Mardie spoke up. Every eye turned to her. "My body shows all kinds of new problems down here, things I never suffered on Earth. Stomach cramps, asthma attacks, migraines, hacking so bad I cough up blood."

Lucifer narrowed his eyes and glared at Mardie. "It seems to me that you are forgetting that you are in Hell. I said you were immortal. I didn't say you would feel good."

Mardie felt like she'd been slapped in the face. She opened her mouth to respond, but Mili put her hand on hers.

"I think your suggestion of examining the internals of the two cadavers for relative robustness is well taken and may be very helpful," she told Satan.

"Then I would invite you to end this meeting and go do it," he said. Lucifer's words sounded like a suggestion, but his tone made it clear that it was a command.

Mili nodded. It was obvious that Satan wanted this meeting over, but she still had questions. Pfotenhauer went outside to have a smoke. Mardie, still smarting from Lucifer's demeaning treatment, followed him. What did the Devil really know about what it was like for her or for anybody else who lived in Hell? The fact was, Satan *couldn't* know, what with his angelic beauty and perfect body. Yet while she fretted, it dawned on her that it didn't really matter what Lucifer knew or didn't know about how people lived down here. Hell had been planned and created by Jehovah to contain the unrighteous. Despite His absence, it nonetheless ran on His rules, making it very likely that there wasn't a damn thing the Devil could do about anything in the kingdom he supposedly ruled. Further, this lack of control was now excruciatingly highlighted by the appearance of a serial killer, a vicious and unexpected foe defying Lucifer and generating more chaos in a place that was already out of control.

And this new reality frazzled her nerves. The possibility that she could be murdered had made being damned more bizarre than ever. The dreadful fact that the killer was decapitating his victims, or burning them head to toe, terrified her. So much so she resolved to work doubly hard to help Mili find the monster who apparently could steal lives from whomever he wished, whenever he wished. Mardie shivered, realizing that deep in her heart she was already steeling herself for the discovery of the murderer's next victim. Her only hope, as selfish as it could possibly be, was that it wouldn't be her.

Chapter Twelve

"May I talk to you about some private matters?" Mili asked Lucifer. The Devil immediately waved away the clerks who'd been cleaning up the ashes left from the incinerated photographs that had lain on his desk.

"Of course," he said, turning to her. His eyes failed to hide the fact that he was still vexed because she had stood up to him. Instead of dealing with it, however, he channeled his anger into smart-ass remarks. "I never married. I never wanted children. I have never been gay, or even thought about it. I'm happy with who I am."

"Thank you, so much," Mili responded, not amused. "My questions concern equipment I need you to procure for my investigation, though I have to say that marriage might calm you down a little."

Lucifer raised his eyebrows. No one talked back to him. And now she'd done it again! On the other hand, the part of his brain that was not inflamed with self-righteous aggravation reminded him that no one down here cared enough about him to speak to him honestly. Not that he went out of his way to encourage it. He associated such overly familiar activity with the kind of pain-in-the-ass behavior exhibited by impudent wives and ill-mannered relatives.

"Are you being cheeky with me?" he finally asked, not sure how else to respond.

Mili answered with a straight face. "I was just pulling your tail."

Satan tossed his head back and laughed. "Ah, me," he said, "the tail. And the horns, don't forget the horns." Suddenly the blithe and charming Lucifer had reappeared.

"Who came up with those?"

"The damn Catholics during the Dark Ages. The tail and horns are innocuous and invented, but the darker side of their one-religion-suits-all mentality wreaked havoc in its day, including the genocide of the New World's Indians because they weren't *saved*, the slaughter of tens of thousands of Protestant Europeans because they *were* saved, but not by Catholics, and let's not forget the countless number of innocents the Church banned and burned because they were scientists, free thinkers, feminists, homosexuals, Muslims, and Jews." Satan paused and stroked his chin for a moment. "I'd wager that half of the world's current wars and massacres stem from the hard and fast Catholic prejudices embedded in Western civilization by those spiritual hypocrites. Dark ages, indeed."

"And the other half? Are those yours?"

"You flatter me," Lucifer responded, giving Mili a slight nod, "but no. I'm afraid that the everyday lies, thefts, gossip, adulteries, murders, and general hardness of heart are almost completely generated by the lustful, envious, and unforgiving impulses of *ordinary* men and women. Sad to say, my contribution to humankind's mess is hardly more than a minuscule speck." The Devil's face drooped at the thought of such marginalization.

"And your minuscule speck is?" Surely with a two-thousand-year reputation for unremitted evil, he had to be hiding something about his role in the world's misery.

Chapter Twelve

"Well, I have bargained for a soul now and again, provided that it was someone I wanted down here. In exchange, I provided goods, or fame, or whatever other illusionary wonder he or she desired so desperately that they'd sacrifice their very eternity to possess it."

"You really buy souls?" Mili asked. Talk about the Dark Ages.

"I do," Satan replied without apology, "for real and for keeps, though on rare occasions I have allowed some of my more successful clients to buy their souls back again."

"For cash?"

"And stock."

"Is that how you finance things down here?"

"Oh my, no," Satan responded. "Hell already has the most profitable banks anywhere in the universe, with our own specie, abundant, stable, and desirable. The reason I want and use American cash and stock is to manipulate US presidential elections. It's probably my most important investment."

"Oh." Mili didn't know a lot about the political system that elected American presidents, but she had read in the *London Daily Mirror* that in the last campaign the candidates had spent more than three billion dollars purchasing the media exposure they hoped would win them the top office in America. She wondered how much of his own secret capital Lucifer had injected trying to influence voters.

"I also invest substantial monies into American weapons development, as well, because it's where I get, forgive my saying so, the biggest bang for my buck. I allocate funds for illegal biological weapons and top-secret stealth projects, and I lend formidable amounts to help warmongers stockpile conventional armor, guns, and ammo. I also allocate significant money to generate rumors about who has what secret weapon, instantaneously sparking fear and hatred in people about what destructive capability their enemy possesses. *Iraq's dictator has weapons of mass destruction.* Now that was a rumor." The Devil smiled contently. "Another blockbuster was *Iran is developing nuclear weapons.* Didn't generate much angst when I tied that one with North Korea, but switching it to Iran punched people's buttons all over the globe." Lucifer shook his head, entertained and amused. He looked at Mili and spoke in a hushed voice, "People find Arabs scary." There was no one around. Satan's play-acting was just for effect. Pandering asshole, Mili thought. At least get your boogeymen right.

"Iranians are Persians," Mili corrected him.

Lucifer waved a hand dismissively. "Arabs even scare each other."

"Why haven't I seen any of them in Hell?"

"Muslims have their own Hell, and their own Heaven. All religions do. Buddhist, Shinto, Animist, Baha'i, Hindu, and so forth and so on. Good on 'em. I have enough work with the Judeo-Christian population." Lucifer's face took on a brief expression of *My God, what I have to put up with,* then looked at Mili again. "So, what requests do you have for me, Ms. Wickett?"

As fascinating as the Devil's perverse revelations were, Mili was not sorry that he was finally ready to talk about what she needed to go forward with her homicide investigation.

"I need a DNA analyzer and access to DNA reference files from Earth's databases. Are either one of those possible?"

Lucifer didn't appear fazed by Mili's requests. He smiled slowly, a confirmation, she hoped, that his connections could indeed be counted on to provide what she needed.

"I can acquire whatever DNA equipment you specify, as well as a proper lab to go with it. And there are experts down here who can operate it for you." Satan spoke easily and with confidence. He was on his own turf, dealing with things he could make happen. It also seemed to Mili that he had made an effort to settle back down after

Chapter Twelve

his *I'm a scary fireball* thing. Perhaps even because of it. "Procuring DNA records, or perhaps stated more accurately, *accessing* DNA records, will not be a problem either," he continued resolutely. "I have people who can get whatever you want from wherever you want it."

"For cash and stock?" Mili teased.

"No. My folks just hack in."

Mili chose not to respond to that bit of boastful thievery.

"I am aware of your success with DNA analyses in the past," the Devil went on, the glint in his eye broadcasting the boast, *What don't I know?* "There are eighteen men and women down here who received convictions based on your DNA matches."

"Yes," Mili replied. "I also obtained thirty-four court acquittals for individuals erroneously convicted, their judgments overturned because of new DNA evidence."

"All righty then," Lucifer said, ignoring Mili's work on behalf of the wrongly accused, "what else can I do to help your investigation?"

"You can show me how bodies are created down here for new arrivals."

"Alas, we lack such a skill. All immortal bodies are made in Heaven. Be they for the saved or damned, all of them are generated there."

"So, no bodies are manufactured locally, as it were?"

"No immortal bodies are created in Hell, nor can they be."

"And what about your demons? I know my intimation suggesting their involvement in smuggling Earthly bodies upset you before, but I need to ask you if there is any possibility that some of them may be illegally replicating bodies down here."

"Absolutely not, and I will not tolerate your challenges against them. I have enough to worry about without my own staff being accused."

"All right," Mili agreed. "Unless I have to bring it up again. How soon can you provide the DNA lab? I am still faced with the task of identifying the two murder victims."

"I will have your lab installed and operational within twenty-four hours, and the DNA reference data you want will be downloaded onto your iPad *before that*. I guarantee it will contain virtually every DNA reference held on file anywhere in the world." Satan folded his arms and assumed the pose of enlightened patron, without whom it would be impossible to forge new worlds.

And in all fairness, it was not the first time he'd assumed such a role, having stood shoulder to shoulder throughout history with the likes of Spain's Fernando and Isabella who, after casting out or killing every Jew and Muslim in Spain, handed over boats, sailors, and bags of money to Cristoforo Colombo to find new worlds to pacify. And what a delightfully hellish crusade that turned out to be! Gold was stolen, land was seized, and ten million Caribbean aboriginals were enslaved, raped, and murdered. It still brought sighs of delight to Lucifer's lips when he reminisced on *how* Spain had explored the new world. The crews and officers of the *Nina*, the *Pinta*, and the *Santa Maria* were all down here. So were Ferdinand, Isabelle, and Columbus himself. Dividends on top of dividends.

"Will I get copied on Heaven's database?" Mili asked.

"Ha!" Lucifer barked, entertained. "Don't be ridiculous."

"Can't hack in?"

"I beg your pardon?" Lucifer said, amazed at Mili's remark. Talk about incorrigible. "Are you trying to tempt me?" he asked. "Don't bullshit the bullshitter, as they say, Mili. The fact is, there are no computers in Heaven."

Mili smiled.

Chapter Twelve

Satan stared at her. Had she known that?

"Just one more question?" she ventured.

"Yes," Lucifer answered, feeling expansive despite Mili's questionable manners.

"Remember that buying souls thing you told me about, and how some folks became so successful you let them purchase them back for cash and stock?"

"Of course."

"Steve Jobs?"

"I wish."

Chapter Thirteen

Mili decided to check in on the autopsies she'd ordered on the two dead bodies. She had assigned them to coroners who had used Scotland Yard procedures before and she expected professional and thorough results. It never hurt, however, to show one's face when new folks were involved. Mardie declined to go along, as fun as it sounded. Pfotenhauer dropped her off at the house and took Mili to the temporary morgue rigged up at the slaughterhouse.

Mardie sat down at the kitchen table with a cup of tea and tried to write for the first time since Mili had arrived. If she could somehow pull words and verses from the maelstrom of emotions she was feeling, maybe it would help her cope. You'd think that at sixty-eight she could just be a grown-up sister to Mili, but Mardie knew all too well that a desperately angry little girl still lived inside of her. There was an ever-present resentment at being forced to be with her twin after so many years, mollified, but not relieved, by the fact that Mili was willing to work on their relationship. Ever churning inside of her as well was the long repressed anger over her desperately lonely childhood, unnoticed, unheeded, and unloved by both mother and twin.

Chapter Thirteen

Mardie decided to focus first on the positives about Mili's presence, and to her surprise, there was a goodly number of them. She began by jotting down all that Mili had done to not only be a respectful, harmonious visitor, but a caring, helpful sister as well. She had insisted on the air conditioning and required that pure water and healthy foods be delivered every day. There were new iPhones, and everything in the house worked or was fixed immediately by the Devil's helpers. It was all quite wonderful. Most telling of Mili's caring attitude, however, was that she had included Mardie in every aspect of the homicide investigation, allowing her to witness things she never would have known about without Mili being present—Satan's wiles, Jehovah's aloofness, the competition between them for souls, Hell's mystery, Heaven's strangeness, and, perhaps more than anything else, the machinations of the charming and utterly terrifying Lucifer himself.

Mardie wrote and wrote, working fruitfully until it was time to think about dinner. Her effort felt productive, even redemptive. But what did she really know? For a moment she considered seeing one of the deans of Hell's counselors, Sigmund Freud or Carl Jung, but fresh sirloin steaks had just been delivered from Omaha, compliments of Heaven, and it was time to think about preparing dinner. Truth be told, she suspected dining on prime beef would probably be better therapy than sitting in either psychiatrist's smoke-filled office.

Perhaps she'd serve a traditional Swiss fondue? She could cut the steaks into cubes for cooking at the table, prepare a range of dipping sauces, cook up a few side vegetables, and end with little vanilla cakes ready to dip into melted chocolate. She thought for a moment of offering special coffee with dessert. She glanced at the new Italian espresso maker that Mili had ordered. It had tall brass tanks with copper trim, and black barista handles sticking out like porcupine quills, their chrome baskets thrust into openings here, there, and everywhere, *plus* there were tampers, cream whippers, and countless other java trinkets piled up around the coffee maker like so much flotsam and jetsam. What a crock. Nix the special coffee. If Mili wanted froufrou coffee, she could damn well make it herself.

The telephone rang. Her old one, not the complicated-as-a-hiatal-hernia Apple iPhone that sat at the bottom of her purse. She picked up the receiver.

"Yes?"

"Mardie, it's Lucifer." The Devil's handsome face materialized on the monitor next to the phone. He smiled when he saw her face on his end. "Ah, your webcam is working today."

"Yes. It was fixed again yesterday. Thank you."

Lucifer gave a slight nod, appreciating her gratitude.

"Mili is not answering her mobile. Is she with you by any chance?"

"No. She went to check on the autopsies in progress."

Lucifer grimaced. "Autopsies? No one told me about autopsies."

"She is following up on your suggestion, trying to determine whether the two victims are from Earth or Hell." Lucifer looked like he was pouting. Oh, grow up, Mardie thought. "Remember?" she asked.

"Of course I remember," Lucifer snapped. "I just don't like being out of the loop."

"May I take a message for you?" Mardie offered, and held up her writing materials.

"Are you working on poetry?" Lucifer inquired, suddenly gracious.

"Trying to," Mardie admitted, surprised and touched that he would ask.

Chapter Thirteen

"Good for you. A respite, no doubt, from your sister's presence?"

"Sort of."

Satan chuckled. "Good. Don't let yourself be overshadowed by her. Write your poems. Mili may shine like a star, but there is still satisfaction in being a lesser light."

Thanks for that, Mardie thought. Might as well have said, keep on truckin', loser.

"Please tell your sister that three of the photographs she viewed last night were scanned into a software application that measures skull structure features and measurements. The program determined a 99.999 percent match between one of those pictures and the burned man's face."

Mardie raced to get his words written down. "The resident whose face matched the corpse is named Pavel Cherenkov. He was born in 1904 in Russia, and had a long and distinguished career as a scientist and professor. He was awarded the Nobel Prize in 1958. He died in 1990, was buried in Moscow, and since then has spent his time down here as a quiet and studious resident. At least until now."

Mardie finished writing down what Lucifer had said. She waited for him to continue, but he didn't. She looked up.

"That's all," Lucifer told her. "Please read it back."

She did.

"Add a codicil asking Mili to call me after she gets it." Without another word he hung up.

Mardie put the phone back on the hook. So at least one of the bodies was apparently from down here. That probably would be an important turning point in Mili's investigation, but to Mardie it seemed like just another random step into nowhere. A Russian scientist tortured and burned in Hell? What sense did that make? The poor man had already been damned for whatever his shortcomings had been.

The Wickett Sisters in Hell

Mardie refilled her teacup, leaned back in her kitchen chair, and thought about dinner again. Steak, vegetables, dessert—oops, she'd forgotten the booze. She'd pull a nice cabernet sauvignon from the Heavenly provisions, and maybe finish up with the apple schnapps that had also arrived with the steaks.

She wondered if Mili would be talking about the autopsies at dinner, or discussing the software match between the burned man and one Pavel Cherenkov. Of course she would be talking about that stuff.

Did bears shit in the woods? Well, not here, actually. No bears and no woods. But the analogy was still accurate, just as Mili's behavior was inevitable. The grim and gruesome business of murder was, after all, the entire reason she was here. Mardie decided on *two* bottles of red wine and upgraded the dinnerware from liqueur glasses to whiskey tumblers. That should get her through a night full of talk about bodies, burned faces, and skulls. Maybe.

"I remember doing this once back in the seventies," Mili said, lowering her fondue prong into the fondue pot. The raw piece of steak sizzled and spat drops of oil. "I was invited to a dinner at the manse of Lord Somethingorother. The Yard Chief was there and some MPs whom the royal family was lobbying for a crime bill to make yet something else illegal. Anyway, his cook had prepared a fondue dinner, complete with self-serve pots, meats, cheeses, oils, and sauces. I had just dipped my first piece of meat, lamb, I believe, when it somehow got loose from its little fork, shot straight up out of the oil, and nailed me in the forehead. That was the first and only time I fondued."

Chapter Thirteen

Mardie looked at Mili. "Fondued. Is that a real verb?"

"Julius Caesar would think so," Mili answered. "I came. I saw. I fondued."

"He's down here, by the way," Mardie added.

"Surprise me with some legendary Roman who isn't."

"Well, believe it or not, Augustus isn't."

"I'll bet his wife is."

"Livia, that old witch? No contest."

"What about Marcus Aurelius?"

"Down here. Pride." Mardie emphasized the word by whispering it.

"Constantine?"

"Down here. Murder. Waited to formally convert to Christianity until he was on his deathbed. Turned out he'd waited a little bit too long. Died before his baptism was finished and wound up getting nailed for disposing of his wife and a handful of his sons."

Mili snorted and fastened a piece of steak to her prong.

"One more guess?" she asked Mardie.

"Good luck."

"Justinian?"

"Down here. Lust."

"Really?" Mili pushed the meat firmly on the cooking fork. "Building the Hagia Sophia didn't offset that?"

"Not any more than building Rockefeller Church in New York City saved you-know-who."

"Oh dear me. I thought he was a born-again."

"He was. There are a lot of them down here."

"Must be a shock when they wake up in Hell."

Mardie nodded. "At first. But they adjust, always scouting around for a silver lining to God's purpose, even down here. They spend a lot of their time staging Biblical reenactments. *Noah and the Ark, Ruth and Naomi, David and Goliath*, and so forth and so on."

"*Lot and his Daughters?*"

Mardie chuckled. "Don't be naughty."

"It's in the Bible."

"Not the part they teach in Sunday School."

Mili lifted her fork out of the oil. The steak was grayish-brown. She cringed.

"It's the same color as a corpse," she said, staring at it.

"Tastes better than it looks."

"A corpse probably does, too."

"Dip it in some curry."

Mili did and proceeded to take a small nibble. She nodded, pleasantly surprised.

"It *is* rather savory."

Both twins pushed cubes of steak onto their prongs and lowered them into the hot oil, resting the long metal skewers against the side of the pot.

There was a knock at the front door.

"Good Lord, it's late," Mili said, looking at her watch.

"I'll see who it is," Mardie said. She looked out the peephole. A thickset man with steel-gray hair combed straight back stood there. He had a broad face with a heavy nose and a square jaw. Despite the fact that he was wearing a black suit and tie, he looked very much like he could have been a boxer. Mardie opened the door.

"Yes?"

"Forgive me for bothering you this late, Madam," the man said in a heavy accent. "I have come to see Mili Wicket. Would that be you?"

"No."

The man frowned. "I was told she would be here."

Chapter Thirteen

"Who are you?" Mardie asked. She could see the man's urgency, but she wasn't about to tell a stranger that Mili was here without a very good reason to do so.

"My name is Pavel Cherenkov."

Mardie instantly recognized his name from Lucifer's message for Mili, but she kept a poker face and waited for him to continue.

"Yes?" she prompted him.

"I need to see your sister," he repeated.

"Who sent you?"

"Important people. Very important people."

"May I ask why?"

The man looked flustered. "My name is Pavel Cherenkov," he said again. "I am Noble Prize–winning professor, and my intentions are peaceful."

"Being a Noble Prize winner doesn't make you peaceful," Mardie shot back. "Last guy I knew won that bauble waged three wars right out of the White House."

"I wouldn't know about that," Cherenkov replied stiffly. "Please, I need to see Mili Wickett. I have information that will aid her investigation."

"And what's in it for you?"

Cherenkov flushed, but answered honestly. "I am trying to spare my body from further humiliation."

Well, all right, Mardie thought. The man had some skin in game. And it was obvious now that Lucifer had leaked information to him about it being his body tossed on his doorstep. But if that was him, how could he be here now? Her head pounded.

The Wickett Sisters in Hell

"Wait here," she ordered and closed the door. She went to the kitchen. Mili had heard everything and was already turning her wheelchair. Mardie moved aside to let her pass, glanced at the fondue pot to make sure that no meat had been left cooking, then followed her sister. In moments Mili and Cherenkov got into a row.

"No, no, no," the Russian insisted, his voice loud and upset, "you must listen to me. You think that because we're in Hell there are no vendettas, that old grudges don't carry over from the life before?"

"Get control of yourself," Mili demanded, speaking just as loudly as the Russian. "I am willing to hear what you have to say but *only* if you get a hold of yourself."

Cherenkov immediately settled down. "I apologize, Miss Wickett. I am not madman and I am sorry for acting like one. I am Pavel Cherenkov, winner two Stalin Prizes, USSR State Prize, and Nobel Prize. I have come here tonight to tell you why the face on dead man matches my photograph *and* my bone structure." The Russian's eyes drilled into Mili's. "It is because that face and my face are one and same." He pointed at his face. "Look at me. Behold for yourself that I am telling you truth!"

Chapter Fourteen

"Dr. Cherenkov," Mili addressed the Soviet scientist politely but firmly, hoping to discourage any more theatrics. "Why don't you come in?"

Mili led the Russian into the living room, and Mardie followed. She did very little entertaining in this high-ceilinged great room (her bedroom was her social chamber of choice), but she had nonetheless decorated it with care, striving for a formal English elegance. There was an Oxblood leather Chesterfield in the center of the room with a pair of matching wingchairs facing it across a glass-topped coffee table placed in between, end tables with Tiffany style lamps set on either side of the couch and alongside each chair, with a burgundy and blue Turkish carpet covering most of the wood floor.

Several mahogany bookshelves lined the walls, filled with literary books from every time and place. Mardie's hands-down favorite was a copy of the first Tuscan edition of Dante Alighieri's *Divina Commedia*, published by the Italian humanist Ludovico Dolce, whose had enhanced his own local fame by deciding to appropriate Giovanni Boccaccio's suggestion that the word *Divina* be added to Dante's original title. The rest, as they say, is history. The great Italian poet had reluctantly autographed Mardie's treasure, expressing his desire not to diminish the Almighty's role as the true author of his work by putting his own name on it.

"You're in Hell," Beatrice had told him. "Sign it."

He did.

Mili followed Cherenkov into the living room.

"May I offer you tea?" Mardie asked him.

"Thank you. Black."

"Please be seated," Mili said to Cherenkov. "Mardie, may I have tea also, with cream and sugar?"

Cherenkov sat down on the stiff sofa and Mili positioned her wheelchair next to one of the leather chairs, facing him. Mardie heard their discussion resume as she left the room. She put the water on for tea and filled a plate with butter cookies stamped into the shapes of British songbirds. How camp. Yet, how wonderful too. There were no songbirds in Hell, though there were a goodly number of opera singers. Rumors had it that the famously rotund performers did a whole lot of fornicating with each other. Gave a whole new meaning to *it's only over when the fat lady sings*. Mardie poured the hot water into the teapot, allowed it to steep for a few moments, then carried the teapot, cups, spoons, silver sugar bowl, cream pitcher, napkins, and cookies all on one large Japanese lacquer tray into the living room and set it on the coffee table.

"When I saw a photograph of dead man discovered yesterday," Cherenkov was saying, "I saw that it was *my* face! Imagine my astonishment."

"Who showed you that picture?" Mili asked him, her suspicions aroused. Someone was either trying to undercut her discovery process or inadvertently muddying things up by offering help she didn't need.

Cherenkov was distressed at Mili's direct question and shifted uncomfortably. "I can only say that it was someone in Devil's office."

Chapter Fourteen

"Someone named Lucifer?"

Cherenkov blanched. For a man who had not only survived, but prospered under the imminently suspicious Russian bureaucracy, he didn't hide his reactions really well.

Have to ask this guy to play poker sometime, Mardie thought, pouring the tea into cups and placing them on the coffee table next to the Russian scientist and her sister.

"So why don't you tell me something I can't figure out on my own, like why Satan would tell *you* anything?"

Cherenkov glowered, but rose to Mili's challenge. "You believe that both bodies found at Lucifer's house were murdered." Cherenkov leaned forward and locked eyes with Mili. He spoke in a whisper. "*They were not murdered.*" Cherenkov paused to let his revelation sink in. "They were disfigured, yes. Disgraced and humiliated, absolutely. But murdered? No." Cherenkov leaned back and folded his arms, secrets revealed. "Simple truth is that both corpses are Earthly bodies that were exhumed and dragged down here. And please, note as well, these grave robberies were not done to embarrass Lucifer. They were done to embarrass me and other man whose remains were dug up and dumped."

Mili thought about Cherenkov's claim while she spooned sugar into her cup and filled it to the brim with cream. What he said made sense in its own horrible way. She knew of other instances where corpses had been exhumed and humiliated as though that could somehow even the score posthumously. That exact same thing had happened to Oliver Cromwell's body after the restoration of the British monarchy and the crowning of Charles II. His moldering corpse had been dug up and hung. So there. She'd shuddered when Cromwell himself had told her about it in a chance meeting outside of Satan's office. He was down here, too, lobbying Hell's bureaucrats to establish a Parliament for the purpose of overseeing the powers of the Devil.

The Wickett Sisters in Hell

"You are saying that the body that we found burned and dumped on Satan's steps is, in fact, *your* mortal body?" Mili asked Cherenkov. "Correct me if I am wrong, but I thought you died in 1990. The cadaver's face I saw yesterday appeared rather fresh for being dead and buried several decades ago."

Cherenkov flushed and looked insulted. "You think that Lenin was only Soviet Hero of Socialist Labor to have his body preserved? Check my tomb! Novodevichy Cemetery in Moscow. See if my body has not been stolen out of its mausoleum."

"That's exactly what I intend to do," Mili replied.

"Then you will soon be telling me that I was right," Cherenkov boasted in a haughty voice.

"An occasion I shall surely look forward to."

Cherenkov grinned. "You have grit, Miss Wickett."

Mili nodded. Damn straight. I was a Cold War kid.

"Before I take my leave," Cherenkov continued, "I will provide you one more piece of information. Don't thank me," he said, waving off anything Mili might say. "Someday you may come to think of me as your friend. I've heard that you hope to find out who the bodies belong to by checking DNA records. I tell you, you will not be successful. Such data is scant before 1990 in Russia, and nonexistent before 1984. As you noted correctly, I died in 1990. I was never asked to provide a sample and other man you hope to identify died in 1974, sixteen years before me. So, DNA sample? Impossible." "You know who that man is?" Mili asked Cherenkov, her heart suddenly racing. Maybe she had endured all of Cherenkov's screwball theories and self-pitying rhetoric to get to this point.

"I do," the scientist replied. "I worked with him and I respected him, even if he was a Jew."

Mili and Mardie both reacted as though they'd been slapped.

Chapter Fourteen

"Please, please," Cherenkov quickly spoke up. "I did not say that to offend you. I love man whose mortal remains are lying in your cattle locker."

"What is his name?" Mili asked, beginning to suspect another fanciful self-promotion behind Cherenkov's boast.

"Name of my dear friend and colleague is Leon Rosenfeld." With that, Pavel Cherenkov stood up, walked down the hall to Mardie's front door, opened it without another word, and left.

"My," Mardie said, getting up to close the door. "That was about as much fun as the fondue."

"Not nearly," Mili said, rolling her wheelchair back into the kitchen, "though I'm going to feel a whole lot worse if there isn't some bloody dessert tonight."

"So what do you think?" Mardie asked, bringing over the cake balls and setting a pot of chocolate over a sterno flame. Mili was already filling a prong with cake balls.

"I think the best way is to dip the cakes for about ten seconds," Mili replied. "Let them cool for a moment, then lower them in again. Repeat three or four times and you will achieve perfect chocolate layering."

"Thanks for the tip, but I was asking for your impression of our Soviet Hero of Socialist Labor, Pavel Cherenkov." She reached over and picked up a cake ball off the plate and began nibbling on it.

"What do you think that award would buy our Russian friend at the 7-Eleven around the corner?"

"You think you're being facetious, sis, but Pfotenhauer told me that there are so many Communist officials down here that many of them are happy to take a job at 7-Eleven."

"Well, I am glad to see that there is some sort of pecking order in Hell."

"The German Nazis work the filling station pumps and change oil," Mardie replied.

"Spanish Jesuits run car washes and detail automobiles. Italian brownshirts sweep the streets and clean the gutters, and KGB and CIA operatives unclog the sewers."

"Really? What about the James Bond wannabes at M3?"

"British Intelligence?"

"Yes, them." She raised her cakes out of the melted chocolate, counted to ten, and plunged them in again. "Not very nice chaps. Should be in the same sludge as their Cold War colleagues."

"They can be found trimming scrubs and lawns."

"Well, that's not so bad."

"With nail scissors."

"Oh."

"Dull nail scissors."

Mili shook her head, then raised her cakes out of the chocolate one final time, allowed them to cool for a moment, then lifted them to her mouth and bit off a small portion of the one at the end. She chewed slowly, then smiled with delight. She extended the heavy-laden prong toward Mardie. "You must try it."

Mardie leaned forward and took a small bite, getting nothing but chocolate, which was somewhat disappointing, as by her reckoning she was a cake, not a frosting, fan. "Yum," she said, dutifully. "Lots of chocolate."

"Yes," Mili agreed, and proceeded to pull the cake balls off the prong with her lips into her mouth one at a time until they were gone. Mardie watched, impressed. If that was a demonstration of how she'd eaten on Earth, Mili must have kept canisters of insulin the size of propane tanks nearby. She immediately began to fasten another row of cakes onto her fork. "Didn't you say there were popes down here, too?"

Chapter Fourteen

"They run laundries—washing, drying, and folding."

"Ouch."

"*Protestant* laundries."

"Ha!" Mili squeezed a final cake onto the end of the prong. She looked up at her twin. "Did you make these?"

"No way." Mardie shook her head. "They were sent by Heaven, along with the steaks and the chocolate."

"My. Heaven in Hell. Who could have imagined?"

Mardie took another tiny bite out of the cake ball she was holding.

"So, what about the name Cherenkov dropped?"

"Leon Rosenfeld. The name sounds Jewish, which in Belgium would not have been a big deal. But for Cherenkov to have fraternized with him during the Cold War and be so frank about his affection for him very much goes against the grain in the old USSR. Maybe Pavel is a bit of a hero after all." Mili lifted her cakes and dipped them into the chocolate. "Would you please hand me my iPad? It's on that itty bitty table that holds your antique phone."

Mardie rose to fetch the iPad. "Don't be mocking my phone. If your high-tech doodads fail, you'll be begging me to use it."

Mili accepted the iPad from Mardie.

"Thank you. I'm going to do a bit of a search and see what I can find on Rosenfeld."

She booted up the iPad and Mardie began to clear the dinner things.

"Are there any more of those divine cakes?" Mili asked, lifting and then redipping her current prong of cakes.

"Yes."

"May I?"

"Of course."

Mardie fetched another box. She wondered why Mili did not seem particularly excited about Cherenkov's information. Had she already dismissed his claims as impossible, that the two bodies discarded on Lucifer's front steps were actually long dead folks who'd been dug up and dishonored?

Mardie set the new package of cakes on the table. She glanced at the brand name. Hostess. Never heard of it. She turned the box to look at the content disclosures. Two solid paragraphs of ingredients from the dark side. This came from Heaven?

"Thank you so much," Mili gushed, reaching for the cakes, "and please don't dispose of any leftover chocolate when we're done."

"You want it saved for later?"

"Of course. Why do you think God invented microwave ovens?"

Mardie cleared the remaining dishes, washed them, and put them away.

Mili called to her. "I found Rosenfeld."

"Coming," Mardie answered. She wiped the counters and hung up her cloth, then went and sat next to Mili at the kitchen table. "Leon Rosenfeld," Mili read from the iPad screen. "Born 1904. Died 1974. Studied physics at a public university and became a professor, specializing in the newly emerging field of quantum mechanics." Mili looked at Mardie. "He was also a Marxist, which may explain his connection to Cherenkov. Whatever brought the two scientists together, they apparently formed a friendship that Cherenkov never forgot. My question is why does he believe that both his and Rosenfeld's Earthly remains have been singled out for desecration decades after they died?" Mili turned the iPad screen toward Mardie. "Here's a picture of Rosenfeld, with all of his parts still attached." A bald, round-faced man wearing a suit and vest stared at the camera with a smirk on his face.

Chapter Fourteen

The photograph looked like it had been taken when he was in his fifties. Rosenfeld's intelligent eyes and haughty smile bespoke an obvious awareness of his intellectual gifts. Mardie wondered what the murderer had done with his head. Without it, Mili was going to have to climb mountains to prove that the man in the cooler was really him. Or, maybe not. Mardie remembered that her sister was about to obtain the genetic signature equipment she'd asked for, and despite Cherenkov's naysaying, DNA could readily be retrieved from the cadavers and compared to samples drawn from living physical descendants, providing a 100 percent probability of identity confirmation of both bodies. Thank goodness that when God had finished inventing microwave ovens, He'd invented DNA analyzers. Mili herself wasn't actually thinking about DNA testing, at least not until she had the means to make it happen. She was thinking of other forensic options available to her in the meanwhile. Fondueing her way through the second box of cakes, she realized that even just a cursory check of the two corpses in the slaughterhouse could tell her whether they were indeed the Earthly remains of Pavel Cherenkov and Leon Rosenfeld. She had attended the autopsies on the bodies, but she'd been looking for clues, not old livers and worn-out kidneys. If what Lucifer maintained was true, Hellion bodies, no matter their apparent age, should possess robust organs created for eternity. If the cadavers were actually the old men's Earthly shells, their organs would be shot. Stress and vodka. She picked up Mardie's phone. Ignoring her sister's grin, she dialed Pfotenhauer's number.

The driver's picture came up on the phone monitor. He was dressed in a purple silk evening jacket and a gold ascot. He stood, holding his phone in one hand and a briar pipe in the other.

"Pfot, it's Mili Wickett," she said, observing Pfotenhauer's impressive attire. "Relaxing like a proper English gentleman, I see."

"Clothes make the man, my mother always liked to say," Pfot answered.

"You do her proud," Mili responded, and meant it. "I know it's late, but I'm wondering if you could fetch me for a quick visit to the two John Does."

"But, of course, Miss Wickett. Anything you need."

"Splendid. And please don't change. You look positively dashing."

Pfot blushed so deeply he almost matched the color of his jacket. "I'll be there in a jiff, Miss Mili."

"I'll be ready. Thank you, Pfot."

Mardie had listened to Mili's entire conversation.

"Are you really going out again?"

"Yes. The more I think about Cherenkov's assertion that someone with an axe to grind yanked both him and Rosenfeld out of the ground, the more I want to find out whether he's right or not."

✸✸✸

Mili returned home after midnight. Mardie had stayed up waiting and opened the front door as Pfotenhauer pushed Mili's wheelchair up the newly finished ramp.

"Welcome back," Mardie told them both. "Some tea or coffee before you venture back onto the road, Pfot?"

"No, but thank you, Miss. I'll be just fine."

"Goodnight then, dear thing," Mili told him, and off he went.

Mili wheeled herself to the kitchen table. "I'll wager you're dying to hear the results of my midnight madness. It will cost you a glass of sherry."

Chapter Fourteen

"But will one glass cover all I want to know?"

"Ha! You're a darling," Mili said, feeling cheerful. "Bring the bottle and I promise to be loquacious to a fault."

Mardie fetched a small wine glass for herself, a crystal whiskey tumbler for her twin, and placed a bottle of cream sherry between them. Mili laughed when she saw the large glass set before her and cried "Bravo!" Mardie filled up both glasses with the aromatic liqueur. Mili picked hers up, held it out toward Mardie, and clinked it lightly against her sister's glass when Mardie extended it. Both women took a sip. Mili took another and grinned.

"Neither body is old, nor are their organs, nor is anything else about them. Plus both cadavers have decomposition characteristics of a relatively fresh corpse, dead less than forty-eight hours. That doesn't mean that they won't match up to Cherenkov and Rosenfeld's DNA, but those remains are not the mortal coils they shucked on their way down here.

"Then what body was Pavel Cherenkov occupying when he showed up here last night?"

"Well, not to be a stickler, but the fact is that the man who came to the house last night *claimed* to be Pavel Cherenkov."

Mardie reached over and refilled Mili's glass. Her own glass was untouched except for her first sip. Mili continued.

"What is stuck in my craw is that if the person who came here last night really was Cherenkov, then either he or the body in the slaughterhouse is actually a Hellion duplicate. Which leads me to what I suspected earlier, someone down here has discovered how to create Hellion bodies."

"I thought all eternal bodies were made in Heaven?"

"Lucifer clearly believes that, and for my part, I refuse to even contemplate that someone in Jehovah's realm might be involved in this. No, if unauthorized Hellion bodies are being fabricated, it has to be happening down here."

Mardie's head started to spin. She reached down and drank some of her sherry. She looked at Mili, who sat quietly, finishing hers.

"More?"

Mili nodded.

Mardie picked up the bottle of sherry and filled her sister's glass. "Were all your cases this maddening?"

"More or less, but the unusual aspects and bizarre directions of this one makes it really quite unique. Tomorrow I'm having DNA samples taken from both Cherenkov and Rosenfeld, samples from their Earthly remains, *and* from the two cadavers in the slaughterhouse. I'll have all six cross-referenced and find out who's who, who's old, and who's new."

"I don't think I understand that last part."

"No need. I was just being smart. Those steps will determine which bodies match, but I'll have to obtain DNA samples from their living descendants to confirm those identities."

"Any guesses as to what you will find?"

"Don't tempt me. I am trying very hard not to think about what the results might be until I have them."

"That takes a lot of self-control," Mardie commented.

"No," Mili corrected her, "just a lot of sherry." She drank what was left in her glass and held it out for more.

Chapter Fifteen

MILI AND MARDIE ENTERED THE NEW DNA LAB, a gleaming facility built adjacent to the hospital. Lucifer was already there chatting with two official-looking technicians dressed in white lab coats. One of them was a surly-faced young man and the other was a surly-faced young woman.

"Am I, or am I not, the Devil of my word?" Lucifer asked when he saw the twins. He spread his arms wide to encompass the entire lab. He was pleased and proud to have delivered the highly specialized installation that Mili had requested.

"You are truly extraordinary," Mili replied, beaming. "Thank you."

"I am told that everything you could possibly need is here," Satan replied, clearly flattered by Mili's words. "DNA sampling, denaturing, and hybridization may all be performed on-site, as well as replication of the DNA sequences of interest."

"Excellent. You've described exactly what we need to perform the polymerase chain reaction analysis, the results of which will allow us to compare DNA profiles."

"I received a splendid tutorial from Maggie Riggins and Elvis Carter here." Lucifer nodded toward the two scientist-types standing next to him. "They were trained by Alec Jeffreys himself."

"The pioneer of DNA profiling," Mili acknowledged. She glanced at Carter, a slim man with red cheeks, and then Riggins, a sturdy-looking brunette whose nipples were improbably protruding against her loose lab coat. Mili addressed Lucifer again. "What else did you learn?"

Thrilled to be asked, Satan was happy to show off what he knew.

"The process of retrieving a sample of DNA and matching it against other extracted samples requires isolated strands of DNA marked at thirteen different locations and compared to the exact same locations on the other samples. Any match that occurs very probably assures a physical relationship, as there is less than one chance in a billion of mistaken identification."

"Brilliant," Mili complimented Lucifer. "I would like Pavel Cherenkov and Leon Rosenfeld brought here for DNA work. I think Cherenkov was probably correct when he said there weren't any samples on file for either one of them, though I'll search the databases I've received to be sure."

"Piece of cake," Lucifer assured her. "I happen to know that Cherenkov and Rosenfeld share an apartment they rent from Karl Marx."

"Well, how nice for them."

"Not really," the Devil responded, shaking his head with mock sorrow. "Marx gouges on the rent and smokes Mary Jane in the apartment above. The only possible upside is that their place is cleaned by Vladimir Lenin, excluding those occasions when he is behind bars for shoplifting. Last week he told a judge that he had taken

Chapter Fifteen

household cleaning products from Hells Bells for good Communist reasons, stating, "The point of the enterprise was the confiscation of new cleansers. I wanted to see what could be done with them." Satan shook his head. "He should have just said he was low on supplies."

"Does anyone down here really care about anything he says?"

"My, yes. Demons *love* to gossip, and I love withholding information from them."

Mili stared at Lucifer for a moment. He was totally serious.

"It's a game?" she asked, hardly able to believe that the Lord of Hell could be so juvenile.

"It's a *great* game!" he cried. "It's wicked fun concealing things the pervs are trying to ferret out." He dropped his voice to a whisper. "Did you know, for example, that these two techs," Satan nodded over his shoulder, "Carter and Riggins, had an adulterous fling and wound up committing murder?

"Oh!" Mili said. "Their poor spouses."

"Oh, no, no, no," Lucifer corrected her. "They murdered each other!"

✷✷✷

"I am not participating, and there isn't anything you can do to make me." Leon Rosenfeld sat sour-faced on a steel chair with a white plastic seat, his black wool coat buttoned up tight. Pavel Cherenkov sat on the chair next to him, dressed in the suit and tie he'd worn when Mili met him. She faced them both, seated in her wheelchair and wearing a lab coat over her dress. Mardie stood in a corner dressed in flare-bottom jeans and a tie-dyed tee shirt. When Mili had seen her at breakfast, she'd mumbled something about being able to remove DNA out of her, but not the seventies. Groovy.

Cherenkov turned to his recalcitrant friend and encouraged him to cooperate.

"Leon. Listen to me. By helping Miss Wickett you help yourself. Your Earthly body was stolen and left down here. It is at this very moment lying on a metal table in a slaughterhouse refrigerator." Rosenfeld turned and stared at Cherenkov. "I swear it's true," Pavel told him, "and this lady is trying to get everything fixed again."

Rosenfeld shook his head vehemently. "There is no way somebody could get my old pile of bones down here. So, tell me another story."

"Hey, buster," Mardie jumped in. "I saw your body. Your comrade didn't tell you that the head is gone. The murderer kept it, Leon, and for all you know he's going to stuff it and put it on his wall."

Mili glared at Mardie and Rosenfeld jumped to his feet shouting. "Why are you telling me that?"

"Details were held back to spare your sensibilities," Mili answered, "and I'll thank you to speak without yelling."

Rosenfeld frowned and sat back down. "Say whatever you want. I'm already in Hell."

Pavel Cherenkov spoke to Mili. "I am Dr. Rosenfeld's friend. May I try again?"

Mili nodded.

"Leon. Act like a man. These people are trying to help you. Have you forgotten how to show respect?"

Rosenfeld was unmoved. He crossed his arms and looked at the holes in the ceiling tiles.

"So you *have* forgotten, eh? I mourn for man you used to be."

Rosenfeld sat, unmoved, but, in fact, had heard his old friend. He looked at Mili.

"Why me?"

Chapter Fifteen

Ah, the question that never loses its sting, Mardie thought, be it spoken by the living or the dead.

"I don't know," Mili answered. "But helping me identify whether the dead body is yours may help me find an answer."

That was the end of Rosenfeld's resistance. Mili motioned for Carter and Riggins to step forward. They donned latex gloves and produced sterile swabs to take saliva samples from both Cherenkov and Rosenfeld. These were sealed in separate plastic bags with IDs recorded with a Sharpie. Then the techs took blood from each of the men using diabetic-style sample pins and bagged and ID'd those as well.

"I got cookies when I gave blood in Soviet Union," Cherenkov said.

"We can do better than that," Mardie said. She pulled a large silver flask out of her handbag and offered it to him. "Vodka."

Cherenkov took it and unscrewed the cap. He took a long drink, then capped it and handed it back.

"Too bad *you* didn't give a sample. There's some left."

"Right," Mardie said, taking off the cap and drinking down the rest. She stuck the flask back in her purse and walked out of the lab.

Mili wheeled her chair after her.

"Are you all right?" she asked.

"Just feeling cooped up," Mardie said. "I need another drink. There's gotta be a bar around here somewhere."

"All right. Give me a call and I'll join you when I'm done."

Mardie stopped in front of a place that called itself the Good News Club. Good News Club? With a name like that there might not be any booze at all, plus there was a big poster pasted on the door advertising Biblical reenactments. Mardie frowned. She looked in through a window. The joint looked as sleazy and forlorn as any other dive in Hell. She opened the door and went in.

The Wickett Sisters in Hell

The lights were turned low and the premises were decorated in pink and copper. Dear God. This had to be one of the infamous places owned by Alex Madonna who, despite his name, was down here buying up as much of Hell as he could, and decorating it all just like this. The Parisians had outgrown the Gay Nineties, why couldn't he?

Mardie walked over to a long mahogany bar and sat on a stool. The bartender smiled and came over. He was an Arab man, with salt-and-pepper hair and handsome Semitic features. He was wearing a yellow Moroccan djellaba robe and a crimson fez.

"Good evening," he said with a hint of a French accent.

Moroccan mother, French father, Mardie guessed? France had occupied Morocco as a so-called protectorate for forty years after World War I. It could have had it worse. The British would have mown down all of Morocco's celebrated argan trees. Wouldn't have been the first time. You could ask the King of Burma what happened to his teak after the English deposed him.

"Good evening to you, too," Mardie answered. "I'd like to have a glass of California chardonnay, please."

"I'm afraid I don't have any California chardonnay," the barkeep said. Mardie listened, but was focusing on his dark skin and dreamy brown eyes. "Would French chardonnay be acceptable?"

"The French don't drink their own chardonnay."

"Ah, maybe that's a lesson for us," the bartender said with a smile. "My name is Bowles."

"I'm Mardie."

"Enchanted."

"Would you consider trying an Egyptian white?" a man's voice asked behind her. "It's a light varietal, pleasantly reminiscent of wines from the newly developed Washington State Wenatchee-Yakima-Odessa growing triangle."

Chapter Fifteen

Mardie turned. A fairly young man had been addressing her, thirty, thirty-five, tall with a long face and a severe overbite.

He smiled at her quite nicely, though, and went on. "The wine is a product of ancient wheat fields transformed into modern vineyards." His dark brown eyes twinkled. "My, how the environmentalists howled. Food production subjugated to the fruit of the vine? Let them drink wine, that's what I say." He winked mischievously at Mardie.

Despite appearing tall sitting on his stool, the man's torso was actually somewhat squat, with his height residing in his very long legs and arms. He reminded her of a spider. Despite that physical oddness, the young man dressed quite splendidly, wearing a white linen robe with heavy gold embroidery woven on the front V-neck, and thick golden hems on the sleeves and the bottom.

"My name is Akhenaten, son of Amenhotep, son of Thutmose," he said. "Or perhaps more significantly, son of Tiye, husband of Nefertiti, and father of Ankhesenamun, the wife of my son and successor, Tutankhamun."

"Nice to meet you," Mardie said, amazed at all the information he had managed to cram into his introduction. Only missing his blood type.

"I'm Mardie Wickett," she replied, and offered her hand. Akhenaten nodded but did not take it.

"Pleasure to meet you, Madam."

"It's actually Miss," she said, catching Bowles's eye.

Akhenaten nodded. "How about a glass of that white I mentioned?"

"Sounds delightful."

"Bowles, would you fetch two glasses? You know the wine." The bartender nodded. "Also," Akhenaten went on, "do you know which reenactment is being presented tonight?"

"*Moses in the Court of Pharaoh.*"

"The one with the snakes?" Akhenaten asked, instantly dismayed. He looked at Mardie. "I hate snakes." He turned back to the bartender. "You'd better bring the whole bottle."

Chapter Sixteen

Mardie slid around on her stool so she could face Akhenaten.

"So why are you here?"

"I like reenactments, except for the one playing tonight."

"I mean, why are you down here?"

The pharaoh wrinkled his forehead. "I changed some rules back when. A lot of people starved."

"People?"

"Temple priests. Almost the same."

"But you're ancient, *and* Egyptian."

"Actually I'm Jewish."

"Say what?" popped out of Mardie's mouth. It was not a particularly gracious way to clarify Akhenaten's ethnicity.

"My mother's parents were from Canaan. My grandfather was Jewish, my grandmother was Jewish, and so, of course, their daughter was Jewish. She married my father, who was heir to the throne of Egypt. He secretly converted, calling Jehovah, Aten, the Sun God."

"But you weren't so secret. I read about you."

"I suspect that whatever you read wasn't very complimentary, nor should it have been. I banned the worship of Egypt's traditional gods, dismissed their priests, and obliterated their names from the temple walls."

"I saw that in Karnak, in the temple with Ramses's statues at the entrance."

Akhenaten's face turned sour. "That little toad. He was so full of hippo shit. My father built that temple, not Ramses."

"And you defaced it?"

Akhenaten sighed. "I was young."

"And self-righteous," Mardie added. "That's a dangerous combination."

The bartender brought the white wine and showed Akhenaten the label. He nodded. Bowles uncorked it and poured a taste for the pharaoh.

"It's Mareotic," Akhenaten told Mardie. "It's brought here all the way from Alexandria. Cleopatra's favorite, by the way." He took a small sip. His eyes closed with pleasure. "Truly delightful." Bowles poured wine into Mardie's glass and then filled Akhenaten's. "She's does business here, by the way, butting in from pagan Hell. Have to say though, she's a businesswoman extraordinaire. She's the one who pursuaded Satan to ban California wines."

"How did she do that?"

Akhenaten smiled wickedly. "How do you think?"

Really. Mardie lifted her glass and tasted the wine. It was the best white she'd ever had. Perfectly dry, yet smooth, a delicate grape taste with a finish of honey and figs. She thought of Akhenaten's comment about Cleopatra again.

"Is that an okay thing to do down here?" she asked. "I mean between Lucifer and an Earth woman."

"Oh sure," Akhenaten answered blithely. "Angels used to score all the time on Earth until Jehovah put a stop to it. Too

Chapter Sixteen

many half-bloods, all completely superior to human offspring. Remember Goliath, the giant of Gath? He was angel progeny."

"He was real?"

"He certainly was. Nine-and-a-half feet of gay pride. Made a pass at David and that was the end of that."

"Are you pulling my shoe?"

Akhenaten grinned and sipped his wine. "Maybe a little. But he *was* gay and he *was* the son of an angel. Want to guess which one?"

Mardie didn't have to guess. "Really?"

"Yes, one and the same. Scripture talks about Satan walking to and fro upon the Earth. What do you suppose he was looking for?"

"That's enough information, thank you," Mardie said.

Akhenaten chuckled again and refilled her glass.

"Is your son down here?"

"You mean Tut?"

"Yes. He's pretty famous on Earth."

"I've heard that, though I can't imagine why. The boy never did anything except hunt and write. Ernie Hemingway, three thousand years early."

"The discovery of his tomb and the vast array of his burial possessions are actually what made him famous."

"Yes, I've heard that, too. When Tut arrived here he complained endlessly about the small tomb his successor had given him. Apparently he'd stuffed Tut into the one he'd built for Nefertiti and appropriated her funeral goods."

"I thought I read somewhere that tomb robbers made off with a lot of that treasure."

"Just jewelry actually, and it was Tut who made off with it."

"He stole his own jewelry?"

"He had it *removed* and brought here. It took three separate break-ins, but he got most of it."

"How did he do that?"

"He bribed some demons."

"That works?"

"How do you suppose those two bodies showed up on Lucifer's steps?"

Mardie's eyes narrowed. "How do you know about that?"

"*Everybody* knows about that. Guess who loves to gossip?"

"The demons?"

Akhenaten smiled, but didn't answer.

Mardie tended to view Hell's ubiquitous demons as busybodies and buffoons, though perhaps she had only encountered the simpletons among them. Demons who could break into tombs *and* dump dead bodies on the Devil's steps had to be taken seriously.

Mili glided up in her wheelchair, surprising Mardie.

"How did you find me?"

"Scotland Yard detective, remember? Actually, I just went inside the first bar I ran into after leaving the lab."

"Mili, this is Akhenaten. Akhenaten, my twin sister, Mili Wickett."

"Pleased to meet you, Miss Mili," Akhenaten said, standing up. "Will you join us?"

"If you're drinking alcohol."

"Does wine count?"

"Only if there's enough."

"There may not be. Your sister's been here a while."

Akhenaten caught the bartender's eye. "Another bottle and another glass," he said.

Chapter Sixteen

"How'd you get here so quickly?" Mardie asked.

"You've been gone two hours, girlfriend," Mili said. She looked at Akhenaten. "Forgive us while we talk shop for a moment."

The pharaoh smiled, understanding, and turned to chat with Bowles.

"I have some news for you. Everything matched. DNA from Cherenkov's and Rosenfeld's Earthly remains, samples from the bodies in the refrigeration unit, and the strands taken from our boys today all matched up. What do you say to that?"

"Hippo shit!"

Bowles reappeared with another bottle of Mareotic. He set down a glass for Mili.

"Would you like to move to a table?" he offered the group.

Mili looked at Akhenaten. "I'd love a table to put my glass on. Will you join us?"

"Thank you, but no. I can see that you two have things to discuss."

"Nice to have met you," Mili said.

"You were *so* interesting," Mardie told him. "Thank you for the conversation."

Akhenaten nodded modestly. "I shall look forward to visiting with you again, Miss Mardie."

Mardie blushed; she wasn't sure why. Perhaps because it was one of the few times in her life a genuinely nice man appreciated her and said so. As sweet as that was, he didn't honestly look like he'd be all that good in bed. Mardie felt appalled that she had allowed herself that carnal judgment. Shouldn't she finally be old enough not to worry about a man's sexual prowess when she met one who found her worth spending time with? Nope.

Bowles led Mili and Mardie to a table with a nice view of the stage.

"Here you can chat *and* watch the show," he said, putting the bottle of wine on the table and setting their glasses on napkins. He smiled and bowed, then tipped his fez and quietly withdrew.

The lights dimmed and music began to play over the loud speakers at the foot of the stage. It sounded to Mardie like some kind of Lawrence of Arabia meets Ali Baba tune. A half-dozen men with shaved heads dressed in white Egyptian kilts entered from the wings of the stage. They assembled front and center, carrying staffs topped with painted cobras.

Mili felt distinctly ill at ease. She leaned toward Mardie. "What the Hell is this?"

"It's called a reenactment. Like the military ones in England, but this one is from the Bible. The actors are going to present the story of Moses challenging pharaoh. You know, 'Let my people go.'"

"These people are actors?"

"Actually, they're Baptists."

Mili stared at her sister. "Pour me some wine."

The priests began to chant an arcane dirge, and Mardie tapped Mili on the shoulder.

"Talk to me. You know you want to."

Mili needed no further encouragement.

"As I said earlier, the genetic verdicts are clear, all six bodies share either Pavel Cherenkov's or Leon Rosenfeld's DNA. That's counting their original bodies still on Earth, the Hellion bodies they occupy now, and a second set of deceased Hellion bodies in the morgue. Conclusion? Someone used Cherenkov's and Rosenfeld's DNA to manufacture a second set of Hellions. Then apparently murdered them. But how? And where? And most of all, why?"

Mili paused when the actors stopped chanting, then knelt in unison, laying their staffs down in front of them. Suddenly the rods began

Chapter Sixteen

to writhe, then reared up as live cobras, hoods flaring and tongues darting. Mili made sure they weren't moving toward their table and turned back to Mardie.

"So, despite the fact that Lucifer denies it, someone down here is making Hellion bodies. I can't think of another possibility."

"Actually, there is one," Mardie replied. "Akhenaten confirmed something that you guessed earlier. Demons not only bring things down from Earth for Lucifer, they've got their own black market. Seems to me there's at least an outside possibility that Earth might be where the duplicates are made and then the demons smuggle them into Hell."

"So Satan would be totally out of the loop."

"Apparently."

"Still unanswered is who is making them. It can't be easy, and why would they do it all just to have the replicas killed on the spot?"

A tall figure in a black robe wearing a white-and-black striped kaffiyeh headdress appeared on stage carrying a thick wooden staff. All the priests and all the cobras watched him approach. Mardie figured it had to be Moses, but nametags would have been helpful. Facing the priests, he raised his rod, lifted his eyes toward Heaven, and began to sing. Mardie thought it sounded like the old Salvation Army hymn sung endlessly near her home, "Onward Christian Soldiers." All in all that seemed to fit this situation rather well.

Moses finished singing, then bent down and laid his own staff on the stage. He stood and watched as the staff thickened and began to move. In moments a huge anaconda rose up, then sprung forward off its coils and seized every cobra, one by one, in its massive maw. Moses reached back down for the monstrous snake. He raised it up again as his staff. He cried out, "Pharaoh, let my people go!"

The crowd jumped to its feet applauding and shouting, "Moses! Moses! Moses!"

Mardie stood and roared her own enthusiastic approval, clapping and cheering. Mili wondered why everyone was displaying such enthusiasm. Moses wasn't freeing any of them. She shook her head and poured the last of the wine into Mardie's glass and hers, then lifted the bottle for Bowles to see as the lights came back up. He quickly made his way to their table.

"Another?" he asked.

"Keep 'em coming," Mardie told him.

Bowles collected the empty wine bottle. "If you enjoyed that performance, ladies, there's another show in twenty minutes. *Jesus Walking on Water.*"

Mardie and Mili looked at each other, then Mili pointed at the empty glasses on the table.

"You heard the lady. Keep 'em coming!"

Chapter Seventeen

"WHAT DID YOU TWO DO LAST NIGHT?" Lucifer asked. His tone was not nice. He was sitting at Mardie's kitchen table, a bottle of St. Pauli Girl in front of him, and an empty plate with the crumbs of a cucumber and mayonnaise sandwich Mardie had made for him. He had come over at ten o'clock wanting to talk about the DNA results and found the Wickett sisters sitting in their nightgowns, somewhat of a contrast to his spun silver robe with black piping. Mardie snuck clandestine glances at it. She wondered if Elton John's tailor was down here.

Mili was in her wheelchair, sipping on a glass of tomato juice with her eyes closed. Her head hurt and she felt cranky. She wished she could blame it on blood sugar, but that excuse was gone. The ugly truth was that she was terribly hungover.

"We were at the Good News Club," Mardie told Lucifer. She was drinking tomato juice, too, mixed with vodka.

"The schlocky reenactment joint?" Lucifer said, as though they'd gone there specifically to offend him.

Mili nodded, but didn't open her eyes. She was really not in the mood for Satan's disapproval. She had found the performances charming and undemanding, simple parables and pageants that required minimal mental investment. Granted, it wasn't Harold Pinter, but who needed that down here?

"Which show did you see?" Lucifer asked, curious and hating himself for it.

"The one about Moses and pharaoh," Mardie answered.

"Moses and pharaoh?" the Devil sneered. "That's about *snakes*, for God's sake."

"Well, I liked it," Mardie said. "And what's wrong with snakes? It was kind of creepy good."

Lucifer closed his eyes and threw his hands up. It suddenly struck Mili what his real issue was.

"Are you portrayed in some of the reenactments?"

"Yes," Satan almost growled, "in several of them. The worst is called *Jesus in the Wilderness*."

"We didn't see that one."

"Well, I'm glad. The first thing they got wrong was Jesus. The actor who plays him is as fat as Orson Wells, and the actor who plays me is as skinny as Monty Burns. And then there's the story! Jesus is fasting in the wilderness and I show up to see what mischief I can do. That part I like. But the first thing I do is offer him some bread. Bread? Who am I, James Beard?" Satan slapped his forehead.

"Then I sweep out my arm toward the horizon and tell Jesus that if he jumps off the cliff we're standing on, it will prove he really is the Son of God because the angels will save him." Lucifer shakes his head in disgust. "As if he needs to prove anything to *me*, the ultimate dishonored exile from Heaven.

"Although Jesus manages to avoid my first two ingenious temptations, I have one more up my sleeve." Satan swishes his silver sleeve in the air. "I tell him that if he bows down to me I'll hand over the Earth. Not Hell, mind you, which I actually have some claim

Chapter Seventeen

to, but Earth! Can you believe that? Of course, he scorns me and the audience throws any convenient pieces of food on their tables at me." Satan shook his head in disgust. "Why not just make Jesus and me Punch and Judy? Ax the inane dialogue and the half-assed temptations, and just let us beat each other silly."

Mardie got up and fetched another bottle of St. Pauli Girl for Lucifer. Mili was sound asleep.

"So what was the real story of the temptation?" she asked.

"Real? It's not real. The whole thing is made up. Pretend! Never happened. Its only point is to make me look ridiculous."

"So you've never met Jesus?"

"Of course I've met Jesus. I'm not a total nobody on the cosmic scene."

"I didn't think you were."

"Well, the reenactment people most certainly do. I've met Jesus lots of times. Up to this day I am required to report to Jehovah whenever he demands it. Jesus is always there, and sometimes he chats with me. Asks me how I am. He's just that kind of guy. I don't know how he turned out so well, considering who his dad is."

"Well, I think it's kind of amazing that Jesus would talk to you, considering that you tried to kill him. Or are you going to tell me that was made up, too?"

"No, that was real. I starting trying to kill him when he was just a baby, and I finally got him when I persuaded Pontius Pilate to work for me."

"What did that cost?"

"Enough gold to bribe the Praetorian Guard to depose the emperor. My money got Jesus crucified, but someone ratted Pilate out and he was recalled to Rome to stand trial for treason."

"And after all that effort, Jesus came back from the dead."

"I know!" Satan yelped. "Can you believe it? Safe to say I never saw that coming."

Mili opened her eyes slowly.

"Well, hello, sleepyhead," the Devil greeted her. "Where have you been all this time?"

Mili smiled drowsily. "I dreamed I was in Heaven. Jesus was there. He told me to go to your house and wait for the next victim."

"What?" Satan cried.

"He told me to go to your house—"

"I heard, I heard. There's going to be another murder?"

Mili nodded.

"And you're positive it was Jesus who told you that?"

Mili nodded again.

"Have you ever seen him before?"

Mili shook her head.

"Then what makes you so sure it was Jesus?"

Mili thought about that for a moment. "He told me that he had a special message for you."

"He did?" Lucifer leaned forward anxiously.

"Yes, about the Temptation in the Wilderness reenactment. He said, get over it."

✹✹✹

Mili sat holding an ice pack on top of her head. Lucifer was gone. He'd left in a grumpy mood.

"Now that you're sober, do you still think you saw Jesus?" Mardie questioned, eating her own cucumber and mayo sandwich.

Chapter Seventeen

"How would I know?" Mili complained. "I was listening to Lucifer yammering about the Temptation in the Wilderness and the next thing I knew I was sitting by a lake and Jesus was there. He spoke to me and I told you what he said."

"I think maybe you went to sleep thinking that stuff."

"Or perhaps my own instincts are warning me that the killings aren't over. Whatever the cause, I am taking seriously the possibility that another murder victim may be dumped soon."

Mili adjusted the bag on her head. As the ice melted, there were fewer corners to poke her scalp. She watched Mardie eating her sandwich.

"Do we have any ice cream?"

"Some plain old vanilla."

"Plain old vanilla would be fine."

"Okay," Mardie said, standing up. "Headache easing off at all?"

"Not really. What was I thinking last night? *Keep 'em coming.* A woman my age shouldn't even be allowed to use that phrase."

Mardie took out the ice cream. She removed the top from the round container and set it in front of Mili, along with a bowl, a spoon, and a bunch of paper napkins.

"Thank you," Mili said, pulling the ice cream container over. "I don't need the bowl."

Mardie put it back. Mili picked up the spoon and began eating directly from the tub of ice cream.

"We could station ourselves at Lucifer's house," she said. "Not around the clock, but we could maintain some kind of watch during prime hours, by which I mean the times when the other bodies appeared, say nine in the morning until three o' clock or so."

The Wickett Sisters in Hell

"That would still be a lot of sitting around."

"I agree, but it's going to have to be done. If the murderer is still in the business of killing, he's going to dump the body there, and very likely during the same time period as before. I think I should talk to Lucifer about getting this started. Maybe he can schedule his security demons for the times we can't be there."

"Good luck with that."

"Meaning what?"

"Those two security demons are morons. They can't even guard Lucifer's gates without thinking they have to be aliens or dinosaurs."

"Valid point. What about asking Cherenkov and Rosenfeld to help us out?"

"Oh please. Asking Laurel and Hardy would probably be a better idea."

Mardie couldn't imagine the two quantum physicists sitting waiting for the killer. It's not that they weren't smart, they probably could think circles around even her brilliant twin, and as Mili had pointed out, they both had skin in the game. Literally. But for all that, something was bothering her. She couldn't get away from the creepy feeling that the scientists were somehow linked to the murders. Mardie shivered. Where did that weird thought come from? She got up and went to the icebox for a bottle of St. Pauli Girl. She sat back down, popped off the cap, and leaned back in her chair. Whoa. It was last night all over again. Sitting on her ass. Boozing it up. Wasting time. All she was missing were the snakes. And the Baptists.

Chapter Eighteen

"The killer is probably going to be armed, you know." Mardie stared at Mili, sitting next to her in the backseat of the Volvo. She wasn't sure Mili had any formal plan for their first stakeout, yet here they were, being driven to Lucifer's house by Pfotenhauer. Mili looked out her car window. She didn't respond. "He's not only a murderer," Mardie went on, "he's probably some kind of psycho, high on pills, or meth, and won't think anything of plugging two old spinsters. Even one in a wheelchair."

Mili turned to her sister. "Easy, girl. He hasn't even shown up yet."

"But who knows what he'll do when he drops in and finds us there waiting for him this time?"

"I don't think he'll be all that surprised. He probably can't figure out why we haven't shown up already." Mili looked out her car window. "Do you think the landscape around here is depressing?"

Of course, it's depressing, Mardie thought, but what does that matter when you're being driven to imminent slaughter by an unsympathetic sister?

"I think *you're* depressing."

"I think you're right."

The Wickett Sisters in Hell

"Well, get over it. You're not the one who's stuck here forever."

"No, that's not it. I'm experiencing some kind of anxiety over not being further along on this case. Everything is confusing and contradictory, and I have absolutely no idea where the evidence is leading. I'm failing, and I don't want to fail."

Mardie was stunned by her sister's admission. She studied her twin for a few moments. Mili's face betrayed her anxiety, but was it really performance angst? Mili had only been here three days and by anyone's admission had made huge progress. So what had she been doing besides working? Not much besides eating and drinking.

"It's not the case that has you feeling off, Mil, it's all the alcohol you drank the last couple of days. When's the last time you had anything to eat?"

"Breakfast," Mili replied. "I got up before you did, remember?"

"What did you have?"

"Ice cream."

"I thought you finished that off last night."

"More arrived this morning."

"How much?"

"Two more cartons."

"And you . . . ?"

"Ate both of them."

"Well, then it's not work or the booze. You're having a serious sugar downer."

Mili shook her head. "I wish it were that simple. I'm telling you, Mardie, it's this case that is making me feel overwhelmed."

"If anyone can solve these horrible murders, it's you. Nobody else has any idea how to do it. Lucifer is standing around scratching his balls, and despite your vision of Jesus handing you a tidbit, the folks in Heaven have been equally useless. You're dealing with a serial

Chapter Eighteen

killer, and worse, a twisted monster who is making bodies just so he can torture and kill them. This is big, Mili Wickett, the biggest case of your career, and I have no doubt that you are going to solve it."

Mili stared at Mardie, and tears began to run down her cheeks. Before Mardie could say another thing, Pfotenhauer stopped the car outside the gates to Lucifer's property. They were standing wide open.

"I don't see the guards," Pfot said, his voice troubled.

Instantly Mili sat up straight, transformed on the spot into the hardboiled London detective that she really was. Mardie felt relieved. Whoever had been sitting next to her feeling sorry for herself had not seemed like Mili, and now, thank goodness, that person was gone.

"Scout around, Pfot," Mili told him. "They can't be far."

Pfotenhauer stepped out of the car and walked up a bit of the drive that led to Lucifer's house. He returned to the car.

"Nada" was his only comment.

"Drive on up. Maybe they're at the house."

And maybe they're the psycho killers, Mardie thought and felt her stomach knot up. Could the next victim that Jesus had warned Mili about be Lucifer himself?

"I see them," Pfotenhauer announced as he approached the house. "They're on the porch by the front door."

Mardie's fears pounced again.

"They're waiting for us."

"Possibly."

"To kill us!"

"Shush," Mili said, taking Mardie's hand and holding it. Pfotenhauer pulled the Volvo up to the front steps. Both red demons were there.

139

"I think we're okay," Mili told her sister, patting her sister's hand. Then she saw what was on the porch in front of them, a pile of severed human limbs stacked up with a head sitting on the top. Mardie looked away. Mili got out and took her crutch. She went up the steps to face the two security guards.

"Why aren't you at the gates?" Mili demanded.

The front door swung open and Lucifer stepped out. He was wearing a crimson robe with a large blue-and-white glass evil eye hung around his neck.

"It's okay. I ordered them up to the house."

"Before or after that?" Mili asked, pointing at the oozing heap of flesh.

"Before. I brought them up here last night. I took your warnings seriously or that might be me hacked to pieces." Lucifer stared at Mili, afraid. Mili wished she could assuage his fear, even if she only mouthed empty phrases of comfort, but she found that she could not. For the first time in her long career pursuing murderers, she knew that she had run out of time.

✱✱✱

Mili leaned on her crutch and stared at the obscene pile of body parts. Mardie stood next to her holding a handkerchief over her nose and mouth.

"Did you discover this?" Mili asked Lucifer.

"No. The guards watched it being delivered."

Mili gave Satan a sharp look.

"Tell me *exactly* what happened," she said, glancing at the two demons, "and explain why they are standing there with the murderer nowhere to be seen."

Chapter Eighteen

Satan was offended at Mili's bluntness, but he told her what he knew.

"The demons were stationed in front of the door, exactly as I positioned them last night. This morning, no more than a few minutes ago, they witnessed a man materialize on the porch out of nowhere, literally out of nowhere, stepping right out of the air itself. He was pushing a wheelbarrow filled with those sawn-up body parts and he headed straight up the porch toward the front door. He was a Caucasian male, tall, very heavyset, with receding dark hair, wearing black horn rim glasses, a black suit, white shirt, and a narrow black tie."

"And he was alone?" Mili asked.

"All alone, straining to push the wheelbarrow by himself. He unloaded the body parts and stacked them just as you see. When he finished, he turned the wheelbarrow around and started back. It was only then that the guards pounded on the door and called for me. It was too late. By the time I came out he had already pushed his wheelbarrow into the same invisible portal from whence he'd come and disappeared."

Mili looked again at the stack of bones and gore, then turned and locked eyes with Lucifer.

"And the demons did nothing the entire time."

Lucifer glared at her. "I told you, I ordered them to guard the house."

Mili turned to the two demons. They looked human despite their outlandish height and skin as red as Easter egg dye. Had they really just stood by and watched the murderer build his macabre mound without even a shout toward the house? She fought down feelings of genuine panic at the thought that Satan's own bodyguards might be part of an assassination plot.

"What is bothering you?" Lucifer asked.

"The demons' story is absurd. I am supposed to believe that a man dressed in a suit and tie stepped out of a slit in space pushing a wheelbarrow full of body parts, then stacked them up on your porch while your loyal demons did nothing to alert you until it was too late to see a goddamn thing."

Mardie spat the last two words out. "Did I tell you I think all this is farfetched? No, that's too kind. How about, did I tell you I think all this is horseshit?" Satan's eyes narrowed and little flickers of fire erupted on his shoulders. "Think whatever you want," he snarled. "I believe them."

"Including the part where the killer mysteriously appears out of and disappears back into thin air?" Mili shouted, fed up with both the demons' lies and Satan's temper.

"That's not impossible!" Lucifer hollered back, his hair catching fire and flaming into a blinding blue-and-yellow sheath of fire.

"Can *you* do it?" Mili yelled back at the top of her lungs.

Lucifer disappeared.

Moments later he returned, appearing in exactly the same spot as before, flame-free and smiling smugly.

"Where did you go?" Mili demanded.

"Heaven," Satan replied in a smart-ass tone. "Back and forth in ten seconds."

"How did you do that?"

"I used a passage through space. Not space as you've been taught to visualize it, an inky pool filled with stars spreading into infinity, but real space, composed of layers and layers of the universe, piled up on top of each other like stories in a skyscraper, each layer containing trillions and hundreds of trillions of square miles of cosmos folded back on itself. There are openings, holes that bore through those layers like a pinprick through a bolt of cloth. I stepped

Chapter Eighteen

into a hole that let me step out in Heaven. There are countless such holes drilled through space, perhaps an endless number, connecting everything to everything else. Using them is called *folding*, moving instantaneously through the folds of the universe."

"Who else uses them?"

"Jehovah. The angels."

"Demons?"

"Forbidden."

"Humans?"

"Jesus, possibly others, but none that I've ever heard of. The ability to see the holes requires an awareness unique to divine beings."

"So if our murderer has been using one of those, is it fair to assume that he must be divine?"

"I have to admit that I've been struggling with that very question myself. If an angel is using that hole, then it can only mean that Jehovah is involved. There is no such thing as a rogue angel."

"If that's true, then God has indeed singled you out," Mili said. "But why would He punish others if you're His target?"

"How should I know?" the Devil cried. "I'm still coming to grips with the fact that He might be trying to kill me."

"Fair enough. But what about the man in the black suit? He doesn't exactly sound like an angel."

"I don't know," Lucifer replied, looking distressed. "It could be Jehovine mockery. You know, the undertaker coming for me?"

"Sick. Would He really do such a thing?"

"No, probably not. But I know someone who would, the Archangel Michael. He's the one who gets God's bloodiest assignments. He slaughtered the firstborn of Egypt and mopped up a hundred thousand Assyrian soldiers blockading Jerusalem, *by himself*."

Mili stared at Lucifer. Could it possibly be true that Michael was butchering Hellions as a prelude to killing Lucifer himself? Acting on God's behalf, no less? Such a scenario seemed to go against every traditional comprehension of God as just and good. Yet she'd seen powerful and mighty humans exterminate supposed threats, even their own kin, stoutly protesting the deed, but approving the act. Why not God?

A Scotland sage had termed it the Joab effect, citing how King David had instructed his commanding general, Joab, to spare the life of his rebellious son, Absalom, yet at the same time knowing in his heart that Joab would hunt him down and kill him. Et tu, Jehovah? Satan believed it was possible, and who knew God better than he? Despite his bravura down here in Hell, it had become abundantly clear to Mili that Lucifer feared God and he feared death. Was Jehovah about to strike the ancient assassin dead at last? Who could know? Not Lucifer. And not Mili Wickett.

Chapter Nineteen

Mili and Mardie took a table at the back of the Good News Club. Pfotenhauer parked the car and joined them. Mili was in a royal funk, unable to discern whether it was truly Jehovah who was attempting to disrupt the balance between Heaven and Hell by humiliating Lucifer and perhaps even plotting his murder. Utterly unbelievable, yet Satan believed it, and maybe with good reason, as dead bodies kept getting tossed onto his porch.

Bowles brought over a bottle of the lovely Mareotic white wine and three glasses. He'd greeted everyone earlier, and this time he winked at Mardie. She smiled at him, feeling a slight flush in her cheeks. Bowles noticed, smiled gently, and went back to the bar. Mardie wondered if she should leave her number on a napkin for him. She didn't know hieroglyphics. No. He was Moroccan. So Arabic? French? She decided on plain old English and a lipstick kiss. If he couldn't read the number, he'd understand the smooch.

Mili poured wine for Mardie and Pfot and rehashed the demons' story of the man from space appearing out of nowhere with his butchered victim.

"I don't get the folding thing, yet," Mardie said.

"I don't expect to get the folding thing, ever," Pfot chimed in.

Mili tried to explain. "I think it must be rather like stepping into a dark hallway in your own home. You know where it leads and where it ends even though you can't see the other side. Whoever is using the opening to Lucifer's house knows it just like that hallway."

"And he used it again today," Pfot added, "dumping off yet another corpse. It's like he's got a bleedin' list."

Mili stared at Pfotenhauer. "My God, that's brilliant, Pfot. The first victim was a Marxist quantum physics professor, Pavel Cherenkov. Next was another Marxist quantum physics professor, a contemporary, in fact, Leon Rosenfeld. They knew each other in life, and they room together here in Hell. I'd be willing to wager my precious glass of Mareotic that today's victim may well be yet another Marxist quantum physics professor from the same era as the first two, which means that both Cherenkov and Rosenfeld might very well know who it is."

Mili grabbed her purse and rummaged around for her mobile phone. She pulled it out and punched in Lucifer's number. He answered.

"Have you had the new body removed yet?" Mili asked breathlessly.

"No. I can't deal with it yet. I'm sitting here working on a bottle of *limoncello* that Raphael gave me."

"*The* Raphael?"

"Yes. He claims he made the *limoncello*. Said he got the recipe from Michelangelo, which, of course, is a crock. They were terrible enemies. Too bad they didn't kill each other back when so I'd have old Buonarroti down here, too. My guess is that Raphael heisted a case from Pope Julius's wine cellar when he was painting his library."

"Thank you for all that," Mili said, careful not to add *shit* at the end of her sentence. "I called to see if we could have Cherenkov

Chapter Nineteen

and Rosenfeld have a look at the new body. I have a hunch they just might know who the dead man is."

"No need," the Devil replied, lifting his glass and sipping the yellow liqueur. "One of the red demons you and Mardie are so unimpressed with noticed that the victim was still in possession of his fingerprints and had a set taken."

"My God," Mili muttered, "I can't believe I missed that."

"Doesn't matter," Satan told her graciously. "We're all on the same team, remember?"

"Thank you," Mili replied, humbled by her mistake. "Pfot suggested that the murderer may be checking off victims on a list. Given the killer's predilection for quantum physicists, I still think it might be worth having Pavel Cherenkov and Leon Rosenfeld view the body."

"Fine, I'll try anything that will help us catch the bastard." Satan drank down the last of the *limoncello*. "What has he got against me? Nothing about any of this adds up. It's all one big nauseating puzzle with the damn pieces getting tossed on my property."

"You sound like Job."

"Don't talk about that guy. I had him completely over a barrel and Jehovah bailed him out." Satan shook his head at the memory. Then he looked at the monitor again. "I'll get the fingerprints run. If those don't pan out, we'll roust Cherenkov and Rosenfeld." With that he ended the call.

Bowles reappeared yet again and filled everyone's glasses.

"I probably shouldn't be drinking three nights in a row," Mili said.

Mardie glanced at her watch. "It's only two-thirty in the afternoon."

"It's night somewhere. *Salut*," she said, holding her glass up.

"Heaven is not involved in these killings," Pfotenhauer said, "if you'll pardon me for offering my opinion."

"Pfot, there are no formalities between us," Mili assured him. "Speak your mind."

"This is mob stuff. Torture, beheadings, butchery, murder. I don't know who is responsible for doing these things, but I tell you, it's mob stuff, cruel, heartless mob stuff."

"Pfot," Mili responded, "did you ever witness such activities?"

"Yes. When the boss wanted to eliminate a competitor, or punish someone who owed him money, or sometimes just to get rid of someone he found annoying."

"But on this kind of scale? Three murders in three days?"

Pfotenhauer shook his head. "No. The only time I ever saw the corpses stack up like that was when we'd save up a load and take them to where we hid the bodies, a bog in Scotland."

"You dumped all the victims in the same place?"

"Same bog at the end of the same road, every time."

Bog at the end of the road, Mili thought. Maybe not all that different from a porch at the end of a hole in space. Mili had not even once considered that Lucifer's place might simply be a dumping ground. But how could that be? It wasn't a bog in Scotland. It was someone's home. *A very important someone's home.*

She looked at Pfotenhauer. "Do you think the person dumping bodies at Lucifer's estate may not know whose place it is?"

"Miss Mili, I've been thinking all along that the nasty chap dumping the bodies here was doing it on purpose, because it *was* the Master's place. But now that you've raised the question about whether he might just be dumping these stiffs blindly, I'd have to say that it's a worthwhile consideration. Although, if that's true, he could have picked a better location."

Chapter Nineteen

Mili's iPhone rang.

It was Lucifer. His face appeared on the monitor. He looked smug.

"Yes?"

"We matched the prints. The victim's name is Dirk Coster, a Dutch physicist and a pioneer in quantum mechanics. He died in 1950, at the age of sixty."

"Thank you. I am not surprised."

And thank *you*, Pfot, Mardie thought. A bleedin' list indeed.

"Please have your people bring Cherenkov, Rosenfeld, and this Coster chap to your office tonight," Mili asked. "With today's appearance by the killer, and the murder of yet another quantum physicist from the same era as the first two victims, I believe we can identify his next target."

"Dear God," Lucifer replied. "You are incredible."

"Then I'll see you tonight?"

"Absolutely. I can get Cherenkov and Rosenfeld over here, no problem. Coster will take some work, however. He's in Heaven."

"Well, get him down here. At least we know now that God isn't after you."

"And how do we know that?"

"Call it intuition."

"I'd call it risky."

"Easy to see who's right," Mili answered. "Go talk to God, and when you come back with Coster, you can tell me I was right."

"If I come back."

"If you don't, then you were right."

Mili winked at Lucifer.

Lucifer did not wink back.

Chapter Twenty

"I'd like it noted for the record," Leon Rosenfeld spoke up, "that I am not happy with being escorted here without any explanation." He was seated next to Pavel Cherenkov, across the conference table from Lucifer and Mili. Satan eyed Rosenfeld, a grim expression on his face. He looked at Cherenkov, then behind him where Mardie, Pfotenhauer, and a host of demons sat. Everyone in the room was silent, watching to see how the Lord of Hell would deal with the abrasive little physicist. Lucifer beckoned to one of his clerks. A tall, thin, young fellow with a great mop of blond hair combed with an extravagant wave over his forehead stepped forward.

"Trump, put Dr. Rosenfeld's objection on the record."

His assistant lifted the legal pad he was carrying and quickly jotted down the scientist's complaint. Satan pointed at the table in front of him. Trump ripped out the page he'd been writing on and placed it there. Lucifer touched the piece of paper and it burst into flame. Moments later he tamped out the last bit of fire, then blew the ashes onto the floor. He looked Rosenfeld.

"Is there anything else?"

Rosenfeld shook his head.

Chapter Twenty

"Good. You are here at the request of Miss Wickett. Your cooperation in whatever she requires of you is—" Lucifer paused and thought for a moment, "—is appreciated."

"I shall do my best," Rosenfeld answered, his voice faint.

Mardie watched what Satan had done to change Rosenfeld's mind, noting that it was pretty much the same way God had responded to Job when he had complained about his suffering. The Almighty was furious that Job had the gall to question him and whipped up some cosmic razzle-dazzle to make Job back down. He did. Sorry, Job. Sorry, Leon. Sorry, human race.

"What about you, Dr. Cherenkov?" Lucifer asked, making sure that Leon's learning experience had not been lost on his colleague. Being the good Communist apparatchik he had always been, Cherenkov knew how to answer.

"I have no issues," he replied. "My role is to support you and Detective Wickett in any way possible."

Lucifer allowed himself a small smile. "Your attitude is exemplary."

Cherenkov chuckled. "I owe it to unending dedication to my development by leaders of Soviet Pioneer Youth."

"They beat you."

"With uncurbed enthusiasm."

Satan folded his hands together and nodded appreciatively.

"Gentlemen," Mili spoke up, "we thank you for your presence here. Dealing with three murders in three days, we have pursued a lot of possibilities, but up until this moment we had not made much progress. I am able to tell you now, however, and declare with great confidence, that by the end of this meeting we will not only know the murderer's next target, we will agree on the identity of the killer. And you two gentlemen, Dr. Cherenkov,

The Wickett Sisters in Hell

Dr. Rosenfeld, will be the ones who'll tell us who *both* of these individuals are."

Pavel Cherenkov blinked in disbelief. Leon Rosenfeld simply shook his head. Mili proceeded to explain her bold claim.

"The first body that appeared on Lucifer's doorstep was missing its head and innards, yet there was hardly any blood. The deceased had to have been murdered elsewhere and then transported to Satan's home. A second body appeared the very next day, displaying graphic evidence of torture, but again, *just like before*, it was obvious the victim had been murdered somewhere else and brought to Lucifer's house afterwards.

"Both cadavers had their finger, palm, and footprints removed. I had the bodies placed in a temporary morgue and Lucifer assembled a DNA lab for my use. It was then that Dr. Cherenkov came to see me and shared his belief that one of the cadavers was actually his Earthly body, disinterred and dishonored, then smuggled into Hell and dumped. He was equally convinced that the other body belonged to his colleague and friend, Dr. Rosenfeld, pulled from its grave, mutilated, and abandoned down here as well.

"Autopsies of the remains showed that they were, in fact, *not* your Earthly bodies." Mili looked at Cherenkov, then at Rosenfeld while she talked. They were completely absorbed by her commentary. "The corpses were too young, yet in a stunning revelation, the DNA profiling showed that the bodies matched yours exactly. I could only conclude that they had been manufactured in Hell, even though the prerogative for such activity is reserved for the Deity alone. That led our thoughts to the fearful possibility that Jehovah might be responsible for these deaths, a harbinger of retribution aimed at Satan himself. Frightening to contemplate, no?"

No one made a sound. No one was expected to.

Chapter Twenty

"Today a third body was left at Lucifer's home and the manner in which it was delivered," Mili plucked each word like a violin string, "changed all of our previous thinking. Two demons guarding Lucifer's house witnessed a man materialize out of thin air pushing a wheelbarrow transporting a dismembered corpse. He stacked the pieces on the Devil's porch and vanished again, leaving in the same way he had appeared. Unlike the first two corpses, however, this victim's fingerprints were left intact, allowing us to identify the murdered man."

Mili drew near the end of her monologue, and everyone was desperate for her conclusion. Both Cherenkov and Rosenfeld were literally on the edge of their seats. Mardie was holding her breath. Pfotenhauer had gripped the seat of his chair. Even Lucifer was riveted by Mili's reveal. She looked at Cherenkov and Rosenfeld, then began to wrap up.

"Before this last victim was discovered, the connections between you two gentlemen seemed easy enough to discern. You were both quantum theory pioneers, committed Marxists, colleagues, and friends. Significant commonalities to be sure. But we had no clues, no discernible connections as to why both of you had been singled out by the murderer.

"Now, enter the third victim. He was European, a Dutch scholar, and a quantum theory physicist like yourselves. He worked in the same post–World War II world as you did. In fact, I believe it is very likely that you knew him, worked with him, and perhaps even considered him a colleague. In short, he was from the same mold as you, and his murder has made it abundantly clear that the killer has been systematically murdering men from the same era and the same scientific discipline, each one a brilliant expert in a very narrow field. Tonight, with the help of this third person, we are going to end the killing spree and identify the murderer. Ladies and gentlemen, I am pleased to present to you, Dr. Dirk Coster."

Lucifer nodded to Trump, and the young assistant went to the front door and swung it open. Standing there was a middle-aged man with dark brown hair and a thoughtful, intelligent face. Leon Rosenfeld jumped out of his seat and ran to him, with Pavel Cherenkov on his heels. There was no question that this was indeed Dirk Coster, their fellow quantum mechanics scientist and respected colleague. The men hugged and slapped each other on the backs, tears coming to their eyes. The three physicists conversed vigorously, reunited for the first time in more than fifty years.

Mardie would have been hard-pressed to pick the saint in the bunch if they'd been strangers to her, though Coster *was* wearing a very well-cut blue suit, a French cuff white shirt with gold cufflinks, a red striped tie, and black dress shoes of a European cut. She had to wonder why anyone would wear a tie in Heaven, but both Cherenkov and Rosenfeld were wearing ties in Hell, so go figure. She watched as the men talked and laughed, Coster sitting right between Cherenkov and Rosenfeld. "Gentlemen," Mili finally spoke up, "a killer is active in Hell. He has murdered three people, and appears to be proceeding down a list of targets. Each of you was on that list," Mili paused to look at each scientist in turn, "but he didn't murder you, he murdered your clones. Why would he go to that trouble? And why the three of you? I believe it all goes back to a single moment in the past, one unique occasion or incident that you three shared together. And springing from that convergence is the reason the killer selected you, cloned you, and murdered you."

All three of the physicists instantly comprehended Mili's postulation, their eyes revealing their mutual plunge into a lifetime of

Chapter Twenty

professional memories, searching for the focal point that Mili was persuaded they shared.

"What I need you to discover is *which* disquieting occasion, *which* troubling incident, *which* upsetting occurrence was shared by all of you? What happened? Why were you involved? Who got upset, then or later? Were there threats? Warnings of revenge? And perhaps the most important question of all, who else was with you when this event occurred? There are no wrong answers. Brainstorm and discuss possibilities for as long as you need. Involve us," Mili swept her arm to include Lucifer, "or ignore us. It is your conclusion that I am after."

A virtual cloudburst of conversation opened up among the three physicists, and though no one assigned roles, Cherenkov took on the function of moderator, Coster made notes on a pad, and Rosenfeld sparred with both of his colleagues, playing the Devil's advocate.

The men talked at length. After a while Lucifer and Mili began quietly using their iThis's and iThat's. At first Mardie thought they were doing some kind of work, but it wasn't long before she realized they were playing hangman, their grins and grimaces hardly those of folks checking their emails.

At some point Rosenfeld asked Mili if there was any alcohol to drink. Lucifer answered, telling him to ask for whatever he wanted. The professor requested a glass of Russian pepper vodka, neat. The Devil arched an eyebrow and asked Trump if that was available. His clerk told him it was.

Cherenkov asked if he, too, could have some vodka, anything *but* Russian vodka, straight up with a wedge of lime. Coster requested an Amstel beer and a glass of ice water. Lucifer looked over at Mili. She asked for black tea with extra cream and sugar. Mardie asked for three fingers of scotch, no ice, and a cold Wittekerke beer as a chaser.

Coster raised his eyebrows when he heard that. He looked at Mardie. "Why did you order a Belgian beer instead of the best beer in the world, a Dutch Amstel?"

"Because Amstel was bought by the Americans," Mardie replied.

Coster shuddered. "In that case," he said, redirecting his remarks to Trump, "may I change my ice water to a whiskey, as a chaser for my Amstel?" Everyone laughed. Even the Devil. With a small wave of his hand, he sent Trump on his way. The clerk returned in short order, causing Mardie to suspect that the boss had a goodly stash of alcohol close by. At least he was willing to share. The three scientists accepted their drinks and immediately went back to their deliberations. Mili and Lucifer went back to hanging each other. Two rounds of drinks later, the men appeared to have finished their discussions. Pavel Cherenkov looked at Mili. She nodded.

"I am not really much of a spokesman, but we had an extraordinary cipher." He held up the notes that Dirk Coster had handed him. "Thank you, my friend. I would also like to credit Dr. Rosenfeld with the suggestion that led to the breakthrough we believe we have achieved."

Rosenfeld looked like the cat that ate the bird *and* got praised for it. Cherenkov went on, "We think we have found incident you sent us searching for, Miss Wickett, an episode we believe sparked all the terrible things that have happened here, an event taking place so long ago it is hard to understand how such hatred and violence could have resulted from it after all these years. Having said that, however, there is no denying that it was a shameful incident, where our words, words of three of us before you, so thoroughly abased the radical work of a young physicist that he dropped his studies and abandoned quantum research forever."

Chapter Twenty

Cherenkov looked dismayed, and it was obvious that whatever he was about to share was truly shameful to him. "Bear with me while I tell whole story. We were gathered in Copenhagen, Denmark, in March 1959, at institute founded by father of quantum physics himself, Dr. Nils Bohr. He had invited all three of us to meet a young scholar whose acquaintance he had made at Princeton University. This man had journeyed all the way to Copenhagen to formally present ideas he had shared with Dr. Bohr in America. We met with him on several occasions, but as sessions progressed all of us, including Nils Bohr himself, became increasingly offended at his ideas. We found them unrealistic and outrageous, so much so that every one of us unilaterally rejected them as fundamentally unscientific. Dr. Bohr led challenges to his theories, dismissing his evidence and roundly criticizing even very way he presented his thoughts." Cherenkov paused a moment, and shook his head slowly. He looked back at Mili.

"And what were new ideas that incensed us so? This young physicist's work theorized that there was not just one Earth and a single reality for each person dwelling on it, but rather there existed an *infinite* number of alternate worlds, possessing an *unlimited* number of other realities for every person alive. Like crazed Siberian wolves smelling blood, we tore young man and his crazy ideas to pieces."

Cherenkov paused again, and looked around the room. "So it was, as I told you earlier, utterly humiliated young man left Copenhagen and abandoned his studies. I cannot tell you at what point he decided to exact a terrible revenge on those who had destroyed his career, but we are in absolute agreement that such a resolution occurred, leading him to commit murders we have witnessed. Why he has chosen to create and kill our duplicates we cannot say, but none of us has any doubt that person who I am about to name is without a doubt murderer you seek."

Lucifer's office was completely still. Cherenkov went silent as well, making the suspense maddening. Mardie had moved her chair next to Mili and was clutching her hand. Lucifer was craning forward waiting for the name of the madman who had somehow manufactured replicas of his enemies only to destroy them, bringing chaos into his domain and instilling fear in every one of its residents.

Cherenkov gazed at the silent people in the room, and spoke at last.

"Man who presented such unorthodox ideas, who we ridiculed and hurt, and who now has reappeared after all these decades as a crazed murderer, is named Hugh Everett III. Find him and you will find your killer."

Chapter Twenty-One

Neither Satan, nor the Wickett sisters, knew the man Cherenkov had fingered. They had never heard of Hugh Everett III, and if he had indeed experienced a career-destroying meeting with these three scientists, they knew nothing about it.

Lucifer beckoned Trump. The mop-haired assistant shot over to Satan's desk. The devil motioned him closer and spoke softly into his ear. Trump nodded and left. Mili watched, wondering what Lucifer was up to. She couldn't hear what he had told Trump, and now the aide was gone. She turned her attention back to Cherenkov, who was waiting to conclude his remarks.

"I have but a few things left to say. Then I and my colleagues will leave you to test our proposition." Cherenkov's face suddenly looked sad and tired, as if confessing his role in driving Hugh Everett III to his murderous behavior had damaged his pride and self-respect. "First, I must inform you that Dr. Everett's theory didn't die, even though he refused to talk about it anymore after Copenhagen. Other quantum theorists who studied work he had published earlier came to accept his ideas. Today, most important researchers in our field use Hugh Everett's work as core of what is now called the Many-Worlds Theory. It postulates what Everett developed on his own and was first scientist to ever propose, *that endless alternate realities exist simultaneously for every person on Earth.*

"Second, Dr. Rosenfeld, Dr. Coster, and I believe that it is not replicants that are being murdered, but rather, other world alternates, actual physical persons habituating a world where alternate Everett has stalked and murdered them. Therefore, truth of it all is that Hugh Everett III is not revenging himself on our clones, *his alternate is revenging himself on us, murdering our alternate selves in his own alternate world.*"

Cherenkov paused to let his words sink in. No one in the room moved, so stunned were they by the scientist's incredible assertion. The Russian went on, addressing the last puzzling pieces of the grisly serial murders.

"If what I am saying is correct, then why did this man go to trouble of bringing the bodies he killed in his world into our world? The answer is actually simple. *He is hiding them here.* Using a corridor he has discovered, which links his reality to ours, he has turned Devil's property into a dumping ground."

Mardie sought Pfotenhauer's eyes, silently mouthing *bog*. Pfot bowed his head modestly. The diminutive mob associate had predicted exactly why the cadavers were being tossed onto Lucifer's porch.

"Third, and last of all, killer is indeed working from a list as Miss Wickett suggested at the onset of this meeting. We believe that alternate Hugh Everett has now killed all but one member of the group that shamed him in Copenhagen, and that remaining soul is Dr. Nils Bohr. Regrettably, there is very likely nothing that anyone can do to prevent Bohr's murder in Everett's alternate world, for that reality is hidden. However, there is nothing to prevent us from trying to intercept him when he returns to our world bearing body of his final victim."

Chapter Twenty-One

Pavel Cherenkov spread his hands wide and spoke urgently. "If you accept what we have shared with you, what Dr. Rosenfeld, Dr. Coster, and I collectively offered as origin of this ghastly affair, you must act immediately, for tomorrow Everett will likely make his last trespass bearing body of Nils Bohr. Then, for all we know, his revenge exacted, he will go back to his world and never return to ours."

Cherenkov took one last look at his audience then quietly sat down. Trump reappeared as Lucifer rose to speak.

"Thank you, Dr. Cherenkov," Satan said, "and thank you to your colleagues. I am sure I speak for Mili Wickett, the driving force behind this investigation, when I tell you that as astonishing as your solution seems, there can be no reasonable argument put forward to void its plain and urgent truth. Let me assure you that if this Hugh Everett from another reality thinks that he can conceal his crimes by smuggling the evidence into *our* reality, we will not only poise ourselves to apprehend him, but will do so with the intent of bringing him to justice." Lucifer scanned the room, looking at his rapt audience. "I am privileged to tell all of you that even as Dr. Cherenkov presented his incredible narrative, I was able to recruit one more ally in our preparation to identify the murderer."

All eyes watched as Lucifer nodded toward Trump. The assistant walked directly to the front door and opened it. For the second time that night, the people gathered in the Devil's office beheld a most unexpected arrival. This time it was an obese, cigarette-smoking man wearing a faded green-checked shirt and a drooping gray sweater, a balding middle age male with a salt-and-pepper beard and black horn rim glasses. He stood in the doorway scanning the faces of those gathered in the room, observing each person, one at a time. Then he burst out laughing, a loud, melodious laugh that echoed through Lucifer's office.

"Well, I'll be," he said, wagging his head and looking at everyone again. "I'll be!"

He threw back his head, held his stomach with his hands, and laughed his exuberant guffaw all over again.

Lucifer addressed the astonished group staring at the amused figure before them.

"Ladies and gentlemen, if you will, welcome to our midst your neighbor and fellow resident in Hell, Dr. Hugh Everett III."

"He doesn't look like the man who was pushing the wheelbarrow," Mardie whispered to Mili.

"Oh, it's the same chap, all right," Mili whispered back. "Tack a hundred pounds onto the younger version the demons saw, erase the last of his thinning black hair, and you'd have this man, Hugh Everett III, dead from a heart attack at age fifty-one."

"If that's so," Pavel Cherenkov said softly, having eavesdropped on Mili's comments, "I have to say that decades have not been kind to young person I met at Bohr's institute."

"Stop whispering," Lucifer told everyone. "Everett ate, he drank, and he smoked to excess. What'd you expect?"

Everett himself nodded, and laughed heartily yet again.

"Please come in, Dr. Everett," Satan asked. "Sit by me." He patted an empty chair next to his desk.

Everett took a last deep drag from his cigarette and tossed it before he stepped inside. He walked across the office to the Devil's desk and took the chair he'd been offered. He acknowledged Lucifer with a nod, then looked at the scientists sitting directly across from him.

"Hello, gentlemen," he spoke in a rich, appealing baritone. "The word around town is that your better halves have been cut down, or should I say dumped off?" None of the men responded to Everett's rude humor. "What has me wondering," he went on, not

Chapter Twenty-One

bothered in the least by their refusal to react to his crudeness, "is how can corpses from an alternate reality show up here, if they, their world, and their murderer cannot possibly exist?"

Well, Mardie mused, Hugh Everett had waited sixty years to take that shot, but it was right on the money. He laughed loudly at his own remark, obviously enjoying the circumstances in which he found himself.

"Dr. Everett," Cherenkov spoke up, red-faced, but from embarrassment, not anger. "I wish to acknowledge that of all quantum physicists who gathered in Copenhagen so many years ago, *you* were clearly the advanced thinker. I personally did not want to accept your ideas because they went against everything I had been trained to believe. But time has shown that *you* were correct. I offer my apology, Dr. Everett, and if you will, I extend my sincere congratulations on overwhelming success of your Many-Worlds Theory of alternate realities."

Everett's grin faded. Cherenkov's straightforward admission had apparently disarmed the big man. Leon Rosenfeld nodded his assent, and Coster did as well, adding, "I ask your forbearance, Hugh, and your forgiveness."

Everett folded his arms and stared at them. He had clearly not expected the genuine regrets offered by the scientists who had treated him so cruelly as a young man. He reached out and picked up the empty glass at his place and glanced questioningly at the Devil.

"Whatever you want," Lucifer told him, answering his unasked question. "Crown Royal Perfect Manhattan. A double."

Trump fetched his glass and left. Mili addressed her first remark to the abruptly silenced Everett. He sat slumped in his chair, as if he'd somehow sailed into emotional doldrums by encountering adversaries who steadfastly refused to be his enemies.

"Dr. Everett, the murderer we are pursuing, who we now believe to be a version of you from another world, has apparently made his way through space several times in order to enter our world. However, when sighted, he appeared significantly younger than you. Can you explain that?"

"Quite easily," Everett said, recovering his verve. "The number of alternate realities is limitless, branching out from the decisions we make and the actions we take, into an innumerable infinity of other existences. The world in which my doppelgänger has become a killer may well have originated from a younger me, yet unlike my Earthly world, time appears to stand still in his, just like down here."

"That other Everett," Mili replied, "has murdered all but one of the scientists who mocked his ideas, *your* ideas, in Copenhagen, and that last person is Dr. Nils Bohr. We believe he has every intention of killing him as well and returning here one more time to get rid of his body."

Everett nodded while Trump set his drink down in front of him.

"There is no doubt that will be the case, and as you have probably also deduced, neither you nor anyone else here will be able to do anything about it."

"We can't prevent the murder; we know that. However, we think that we may be able to intercept him when he comes back to our world again."

Everett took a sip from his bourbon, let himself savor the fine alcohol, then drank down the entire contents of the glass. In a moment Trump had fetched it and was off for another.

"Why?" Everett asked Mili. "Why would you want to do that? With Bohr's demise, it would seem likely that my evil twin, if you will forgive the cliché, should be done with his killing."

Chapter Twenty-One

"You don't know that, and neither, unfortunately, do we."

"And if you do capture the murderer, what will you do with him? Imprison him for said murders? Execute him for those crimes?" Everett raised his thick eyebrows. "On whose authority?"

Mili couldn't answer Everett's questions. She had talked about capturing the killer and punishing him, but the truth was that neither she nor Lucifer had ever discussed any contingencies pending the actual capture of the murderer. By failing to plan properly, she may well have put herself and everyone around her in danger. What if the killer came armed? Mardie was convinced that he would be. What if he shot her or Mardie or even Lucifer? Was such a nightmare scenario possible in their universe, likely ruled by different physical laws than his own? Taking a bullet in her chest from the folding man would not be the way she'd choose to find out. She looked at Hugh Everett again. He was holding the fresh Crown Royal Perfect Manhattan double that Trump had delivered, still waiting for her to answer. In fact, everyone in the room was waiting for her to respond.

It was going to be a long night.

Chapter Twenty-Two

Pavel Cherenkov, Leon Rosenfeld, and Dirk Coster left Lucifer's office after midnight. Each man told Hugh Everett goodbye and extended his hand. Everett did not respond, nor shake hands. Instead he asked Trump if he could have another double. His sixth. Trump glanced at Satan, who shooed him on his way with a wave of his hand. Mardie rose from her seat and sat down next to Everett. He looked at her, surprised. She asked him what in the blazes a Crown Royal Perfect Manhattan was. Lucifer caught Mili's eye and nodded his head toward the front door.

"Is something wrong?" she asked him when they were outside. Despite hours of arguing about what to do when the killer entered their world again, no consensus had been reached. Now she was hoping against hope that Lucifer was not going to take Everett's jaded advice and forbid her from trying to intercept or detain the murderer.

"Nothing is wrong," Lucifer assured her. "I wanted to tell you that what you accomplished here tonight will start to set things back on their way to goddamn normal."

Mili looked at the Devil, surprised at his swearing, then realized that he actually hadn't. He watched Mili work that out, then grinned when she wagged a finger at him.

Chapter Twenty-Two

"You bugger," she told him. "So what's up?"

"I have to go back to Jehovah regarding the fate of alternate Hugh Everett. We can talk about what we're going to do with him until we're as blue in the face as a Moroccan jinn, but the fact is Jehovah holds the power and will make the decision."

"What are you going to ask Him?"

"I'm not going to ask Him anything. I will *tell* Him what we have observed, and allow Him to rule on mad Everett's fate."

"He's not mad," Mili protested, "and if you say that, he may get some kind of clemency."

"Which is not your business. My absence should be brief, and in the interim I have a bit of reading for you. When you first arrived, you asked for some particular information. I would have passed it on earlier, but acting in my own self-interest, I withheld it, thinking it might sidetrack you from your work down here."

Mili remembered precisely what she had asked for, details about Mardie's death and damnation. It had seemed important when she had asked. Now she wasn't sure. She had seen the generous and decent person her twin had turned out to be. She enjoyed her company. She, perhaps, even loved her. On the other hand, she didn't have to share anything she learned with her twin. After forty years at Scotland Yard, her head was full of other people's secrets. Why not Mardie's, too?

"I'll take the file."

"There are actually two files. You asked for information concerning Mardie, and also your father, Morgan James Wickett."

"He's down here, isn't he?"

"Yes. He wasn't a particularly bad man during his life on Earth, save for one glaring weakness, as they say. Unfortunately for him, that single flaw got him murdered *and* damned."

Mili looked directly into Lucifer's blue eyes. They were as cold as Kilimanjaro's glacier.

"Do the contents of the two files relate to each other, besides the obvious biological link between father and daughter?"

"Are you looking for a spoiler?" Satan responded, keeping a poker face.

"No," Mili confessed. "I would like to have Mardie's file, but may I wait for now on my father's?"

"Your choice." There was a moment of awkward silence, then Lucifer turned the conversation back to the business at hand. "Part of hustling Everett over here so quickly tonight required my commitment to him that he could view the cadavers stored in the slaughterhouse locker."

Mili frowned. "What? Is he after some kind of sick vicarious fix?"

"Possibly," Satan shrugged. Hell was full of such people. It was the one place no one bawled you out for it. "Although the reason he gave is that he believes the Hugh Everett from far, far away may have engaged in a bit of sadistic mischief with their bodies, secretly encrypting messages on their cadavers."

"Well, that's a necromantic perversion I haven't come across before," Mili replied, revolted at the thought. "Why would he want to see those?"

"I got the feeling that our Everett, and I use *our* in the most general and neutral way possible, thinks that he may be the only person smart enough down here to find them."

"Well, that I have to see. I'll have Pfot swing by the morgue on the way to your house tomorrow morning, unless Dr. Everett has an irrepressible hankering to see dead people tonight."

"I think his irrepressible hankerings at the moment are limited to drink, smokes, and possibly your sister."

Chapter Twenty-Two

Mili looked back through the open door. Mardie and Everett were now sitting side by side downing Crown Royal Perfect Manhattan doubles like they were tequila poppers. She looked back at Lucifer.

"When you talk to Jehovah about the alternate Everett, what are you going to tell Him?"

Satan looked into Mili's eyes. He didn't like being asked about his plans by anyone. Even having to reveal his thoughts to the Almighty Himself irritated him, but with God he had no choice. Maybe he didn't with Mili, either. She could have declined when he had reached out for her help. Who, after all, would give up Heaven's pleasant hours to search for a murderer in Hell? Yet she had done so. And she performed brilliantly, scoping out the killer even though he resided in a totally other reality. He couldn't have done that. Yet Mili Wickett had, God bless her. He told her what she wanted to know.

"I am inclined to think that Everett is correct in supposing that Bohr will be the murderer's last victim, and that after dumping his body he'll go back to wherever, forever. Maybe that's as good as it gets."

Mili shook her head. She had learned as a detective that serial killers rarely ever found a place to stop.

"The alternate Hugh Everett will have killed four people when he's done with Bohr. If he is anything like the Hugh Everett getting plastered with my sister, he's had a lot of years to offend folks and be offended in turn."

Lucifer understood immediately. "The makings of an infinite number of lists," he murmured.

"Precisely my worry."

Satan nodded. "I will propose to Jehovah that we be allowed to attempt to capture the killer for *His* disposition, or if circumstances demand it, permission to eliminate him ourselves. I'll alert my security demons to be armed and ready."

"Tomorrow morning."

"Yes, tomorrow morning. I got that, Mili."

"Just being sure. Can your demons move fast?"

"Did you see the albino twins in the *Matrix* movies?"

"Yes. As I recall they were outsmarted and blown up by the good guys."

Lucifer frowned. "I was trying to make a point. My boys are as fast as those *Blancos*."

"A lot of good it did them. If your demons can't move fast enough to cuff our visitor before he reacts, *they* will mostly likely be dead, along with you and me."

"Would you prefer that they just point and shoot?"

"There's a lot to be said for that, but my bet is that your demons have never actually fired a gun."

"Thank you for your continued confidence."

"In four decades of service to the queen, I was never wounded," Mili said, ignoring the Devil's I'm Unhappy face. "I see no reason to make an exception now just because I'm dead."

"You're rather funny when you want to be."

"Who's being funny? As bad as I look, I want to look *exactly* like this when everything is over tomorrow."

Mardie and Hugh Everett came outside. Mili could see that her sister was feeling no pain. Everett's eyes were blurry from the booze, but still wary. Mili thought that perhaps the only thing the big fellow had ever felt was pain. Much to her surprise she felt pity well up inside for him.

"We're going to the Good News Club," Mardie said. "Hugh's never been. We called and they're doing *Samson and Goliath*."

Chapter Twenty-Two

Lucifer grinned like the dickens. Mili did not.

"You're already inebriated, dear one," she told Mardie. Her tone didn't sound like *dear one*.

"And just for the record, it's not *Samson and Goliath*."

"But wouldn't it be grand if it was?" Satan couldn't help but remark. "Finally, a happy ending for both of those boys."

Everett chuckled, and lit up a cigarette.

"And next could be *Ruth and Delilah*," Mardie added, building on Lucifer's innuendo, then laughed uncontrollably thinking about it. Everett joined right in. Mili didn't think any of it was funny in the least.

"You might want to take your Bibles," Mili told them. Mardie and Hugh laughed all the harder. Waving happily, they set out for the club.

"May I ask Pfotenhauer to drive them?" Mili asked Lucifer as she watched them wander off.

"No need. They'll be fine. The walk might even sober them up a bit."

"If they don't stop at another bar along the way."

"Bye, kids," Mardie called, turning and waving.

Lucifer waved. "Be good."

Mardie laughed, and waved again.

Mili shook her head. "Did you see how much those two drank in the few minutes that Everett was here?"

"Oh be nice. We all have our issues."

"Yes, or you'd be very lonely down here."

Lucifer smiled good-naturedly.

"Speaking of down here, I'll go inside and retrieve Mardie's folder for you."

"I'll come along," Mili replied, "and I decided I would like the one on my father, too."

Mili rolled her wheelchair up the ramp Lucifer had ordered installed for her and followed him across the office.

He took two folders out of a drawer in his desk and set them on top.

"And you're sure you want them both?"

"Yes. The truth shall set you free, remember?"

"Not from Hell it won't."

"In that case, could you push that bottle of Crown Royal over here?"

Satan did so, setting an unused glass next to it.

"May I read these here?"

"Be my guest. I have to make a visit to the Vatican."

"Is that your sarcastic way of referring to Heaven?"

"No. That's my sarcastic way of referring to the toilet." He waved Trump over. "Her wish is your command," he told him and was gone.

"Would you pour me some of this bourbon, please?" Mili asked.

"Would you like ice?" Trump asked, efficient and obliging as always.

"Yes, thank you."

Trump fixed Mili her drink, and then crossed the room and sat at his own desk, still available if she should need him again. Mili separated the two folders and set them side-by-side. She opened the one labeled *Wickett, Mardell Marion*, and pulled out the sheet of paper that was inside. She put it on top of the folder. Then she opened the other, *Wickett, Morgan James*. She removed that sheet of paper and put it on top of that folder.

Mili read her father's name again. She had very few memories of him, even though he had lived with the family until the

Chapter Twenty-Two

girls had turned sixteen. He was a tall, quiet man, who'd worked as a laborer of some kind during the day and drank in neighborhood pubs at night. The only time Mili ever really saw him was when he was having tea at the kitchen table before leaving for work. He would smile kindly, but he never spoke to her other than to wish her good morning. She never saw him converse with Mardie, or their mother, not even to utter a discontented word, which seemed odd to her. Even as a girl, it had been obvious that her parents had a troubled match. Near the end of her last year in school, Mardie announced that she was leaving home. No one tried to stop her. In fact, Mili was sure that no family member knew or cared where she went.

Weeks later her father left as well, only unlike Mardie, he never shared his intentions to go; he just left and never came back. Mili had always harbored secret thoughts that something had happened to him, something terrible, as he left all of his clothes and personal possessions behind. Even runaways take their toothbrush. He had not taken a thing. What had happened to Morgan Wickett? No one ever knew, and truth be told, Mili and her mother never spoke about his absence.

There wasn't, after all, very much to miss.

And now he was down here. He'd had one glaring weakness, Lucifer said, and it got him murdered. And damned. Mili shuddered involuntarily. Was a sixth sense warning her not to look at the paper that lay on top of the folder? She stared at it, hesitated a moment longer, then began to read.

The Wickett Sisters in Hell

Wickett, Morgan James
February 7, 1919–February 16, 1957

- Cause of death—Cardiac arrest due to blood loss from multiple knife punctures to the chest.

- Cause of damnation—Repeated acts of consensual incest with one of his daughters. Rape of the same before being murdered.

Mili looked away from the paper. She literally started choking at the horror. She forced herself to keep control, to take some deep breaths, and reminded herself that she was a professional reading an official document. Nothing more. Not yet.

Repeated acts of incest she read again. With Mardie. Avenging herself and her unhappiness on her mother in the most terrible way imaginable. Until something changed. She must have refused her father's advance one night and he forced himself on her anyway. He'd raped his own daughter. Mili closed her eyes tight for a moment and forced herself to breathe deeply again.

She opened her eyes and looked at the paper on top of Mardie's folder. She knew what its contents would be. She read it anyway.

Chapter Twenty-Two

Wickett, Mardell Marion
August 21, 1941–June, 2009

- Cause of death—Respiratory failure, chronic obstructive pulmonary complication from emphysema.

- Cause of damnation—Repeated acts of consensual incest with biological father. Murder of same.

Incest. Rape. Murder. Between a father and his child. Between *her* father and *her* sister. Whatever Mili had expected, it couldn't have been worse than this. Mili put both reports back in their folders.

Trump returned and filled her empty glass with bourbon and ice. She drank it down, and then another. Lucifer reappeared. He sat down in his desk chair and looked at her.

"Do you want to talk?" he asked.

Mili shook her head. "I need another place to stay. Please have Pfot take me to Mardie's house so I can gather my things."

Lucifer studied her face. It was grim, yet sad, an expression that cut into his heart.

"Mili, you have only read the bare bones summaries of Morgan's and Mardie's deaths and judgments. You're an investigator. You know that's not all there is. What about their histories, their emotional states of being, their motivations? At the very least I think you should tell Mardie what you've learned and speak to her before you do this."

Mili glanced up at Lucifer. Her face was expressionless, as though he hadn't even spoken to her. "May I stay at your house? It would be the ideal place to wait for the alternate Hugh Everett."

The Devil looked at Mili for a long time without answering. Her eyes were veiled, her jaw was clenched, and her face was set with an iron determination, waiting for his permission no matter how long it took him to grant it. He gave her what she wanted.

"Of course you may stay. Pfot will take you when you're ready. Use any bedroom you wish." With that, Lucifer stood up.

"Big day tomorrow," Mili said, turning toward the front door.

Lucifer watched the crippled old woman roll her wheelchair out of his office. Yes, he thought, it will be, but whatever happens it's not going to have a happy ending. Not for the Wickett sisters in Hell, anyway.

Chapter Twenty-Three

The bars in Hell didn't close at two o'clock in the morning. What would be the point of trying to consume an endless number of Royal Crown Perfect Manhattans if, in fact, there was an end? At least that's how Hugh Everett III presented it to Mardie. Sitting in a booth across from the big man, she failed to see exactly how his logic stuck together. But then that might have been due to the endless number of Crown Royal Perfect Manhattans they'd already consumed.

"Say what you want," Mardie told him, laughing drunkenly. "This is my last one no matter what time it is." She pointed at her drink. Everett grinned and looked at his watch.

"It's only four thirty. The night is young!"

"No, the night is shot to Hell."

"Well, that's true of every night considering where we are" was Hugh's comeback.

Mardie laughed and took a sip of her Crown Royal. She couldn't taste anything anymore, but the chilled bourbon felt comforting on her tongue. She looked at Hugh. He was a big man, but not sloppy. He was well-groomed and had nice hands. He did smoke a lot, but since it had already killed him once, it was unlikely to do so again.

Smoking had killed her too, but unlike Everett, she had no interest in running any more smoke through her lungs. She took another drink of her Manhattan. Running liquor through her kidneys, however, was still acceptable.

"Do you have friends down here?" she asked.

Hugh looked at her for a long moment, as if pondering the term.

"I have a lot of social friends, which is great. I'm not a touchy-feely guy, but I like to go drinking, play cards, or sit in a club and listen to music with my buddies." Everett was relaxed, not drunk, and smiled at the pleasant associations he had just conjured up. "Every one of my friends is an old chum from Earth. I met most of them developing collateral damage scenarios for the Pentagon. I had good times with them there, and I'm having good times with them here."

"What *kind* of scenarios?"

"We constructed various battle plans for the generals and then projected how many civilian casualties could be expected."

"You figured out how many dead folks there'd be?"

"Yes, and not just dead—injured, crippled, maimed, orphaned, yada, yada, yada."

"That is so foul."

"Not really. It's a necessary science and a lot more practical than quantum physics."

"Can't argue with that," Mardie agreed. She looked into Hugh's eyes. The man looked back. He was not shy. In fact, she loved his super-confident bearing and attitude. Her own father had been a mollycoddle despite being a blue-collar laborer. "Why did you let those bullies in Copenhagen make you quit your studies?"

Everett lit up a cigarette and answered. "I didn't have hurt feelings, if that's what you're asking. The fact is, I knew they were wrong and that I was right. But they were absolutely the top men in the field,

Chapter Twenty-Three

and I knew that if I didn't think like them I was never going to get a position anywhere. Who was going to hire a guy that Nils Bohr thought was nuts?" Hugh drew on his cigarette. The tip glowed as he inhaled. "Just the same, I can't believe an alternate *me* would kill him or any of the other fellows. And not just kill. He did *awful* things to them."

Mardie shivered at her own memories of the tortured and murdered bodies. Brrr. She looked at Everett's face. "Yet isn't he supposed to be exactly like you?"

"I hope not. It's true that we were identical when the split into alternate realities occurred, but something twisted him after we became separate entities. Who knows what happened?"

Everett took another drag on his cigarette, then ground it out in the ashtray. Suddenly his face lit up. "Hey, wouldn't that be some investigation? How and why do alternates evolve differently, world by world? That would involve so many disciplines, physics, psychology, sociology, a host of environmental and political factors, culture, language, religion, by God, it would be an endless field of exploration." Hugh's expression turned thoughtful. "But that's not for me, I'm afraid. It will have to be someone alive and kicking on terra firma or terra wherever, sorting out the tangle of threads when communications between alternate realities becomes possible."

"Why couldn't you do it down here? I mean, really. Nothing would get in your way. It would be easy to get any data you wanted from Earth, and I suspect Lucifer might know a lot more about how to contact alternate worlds than he lets on."

Hugh Everett stared at Mardie. "You're awesome."

"You're only saying that because I can drink more than you."

Everett roared with laughter. The melodious sound brought smiles to everyone's faces in the bar. He grinned happily at Mardie.

"No, really. You're something else."

Mardie blushed. Was the big guy coming on to her? She was not quite ready for that, though she appreciated his willingness to make her feel special.

"Aren't you married?" she asked.

"*Was* married. Nice woman. Never talked. We had a couple of great kids, a girl and a boy. They never talked either."

"That's not how I heard it."

"What are you talking about?"

"Your son thinks that *you* were the one who never talked. That you'd come home from work, sit by yourself at the table smoking and drinking, and then go out with your friends. He never heard you laugh until someone played a tape of you and your buddies hanging out at a lounge."

Everett didn't respond. He smoked his cigarette and fiddled with his glass. Was he deep in thought, Mardie wondered, or just mired in lies and guilt? Hugh looked at her again.

"I could be wrong," he said. "It's hard to remember so long ago. I always believed that Mark never talked to me, but I might be excusing my own poor parenting. How did you find out what you just told me? Do you know him?"

"No, not personally. But I've been to his concerts and I watched a television special on him and he talked about growing up with you as his father. You're very famous now. And so is he."

"You said you've been to his concerts?"

"He's a rock musician."

"Well, I'll be. I remember that it seemed like he was always in his room pounding away on his drums."

"He's got a lot of fans."

"Good for him. A rocker." Everett went silent, keeping his thoughts company.

Chapter Twenty-Three

Hugh had the bartender call two taxis. He put Mardie in one and paid the driver. He leaned in through the open car window and gave her a light kiss on the cheek.

"Thank you, Hugh," she whispered sleepily. "I'll see you in a few hours."

"That you will, Lassie. A great night, followed by a great morning. God, I love living in this place."

Mardie chuckled, blew him a kiss, then closed her eyes and slept all the way home. She walked up the front steps, surprised that the porch light was off, but that all the inside lights were on. Was Mili still up? Opening the door, she called out to her. Mili didn't answer. Mardie walked down the hall to her bedroom. "Mili?" she called out again. She stepped in the bedroom. The bed was made. She went to the living room, and she looked in the kitchen. Mili was not home. Mardie went back to the bedroom and saw that her sister had removed all of her things. Except for two pieces of paper she'd placed on top of the bedroom desk.

Mardie picked one up and looked at it. Oh my God, she thought, stunned, and dropped the paper. She grabbed the phone and called Pfotenhauer. Ten minutes later he was driving her to Satan's home.

Mardie approached the two demons guarding Lucifer's house.

"Get out of my way," she snapped, trying to force her way between them.

They moved next to each other, blocking her path with two huge guns they were holding.

She pushed against the imposing weapons. The demons stood firm.

Mardie looked at the guns. They were long and sleek, science fiction rifles with thick white barrels and massive chrome firing blocks.

"What are those?" she cried, frustrated.

"Da.Dooms," one of the guards answered. "Machine guns smuggled down from South Korea. They use cameras and thermal imaging to take a man out two miles away, even in the dark of night."

"And you have these because?"

"Because of the man with the wheelbarrow."

"Who you are going to shoot without needing cameras or thermal imaging because he'll be standing all of ten feet away."

"Yeah. Imagine how messed up he's gonna be."

Mardie pushed against the guard's arm.

"Let me through."

Both demons leveled their weapons at Mardie.

"Do it and I'll personally burn your bodies after Satan pulls them apart limb from limb," a loud voice shouted behind them.

The demons turned to see Mili leaning on her crutch, dressed only in her nightgown.

"Get out of the way," she commanded. The demons lowered their weapons and separated. Mili stared at Mardie. "I know why you're here and I don't want to talk to you," she said. "You're a whore and a murderer. It makes me sick just to set my eyes on you."

"I'm your sister," Mardie cried out, trying to fight back her tears, "and whatever you found out, the real reason you're angry is because you care about me."

"And why do you think that?"

"Because you know *I* care about you, and I don't want to lose you again!"

Chapter Twenty-Three

Mili stood still and stared at her sister. Her long career as a London detective had made her accept the fact that evil circumstances could drive even a decent person to commit terrible deeds. Possessed by jealousy, hatred, or uncontrollable fury, men and women who'd never hurt anyone in their lives were suddenly capable of perpetrating appalling crimes, their consciences snuffed out by their desire for revenge, punishment, or blood. Mili was willing to put the murder of her father in that category. But not the incest. That was another thing. Even as an older woman, Mardie still wore her sexuality openly, favoring tight jeans, high heels, sheer silk blouses that clung to her breasts, and she'd dressed that way ever since she'd first started spreading her legs for schoolboys who'd sneak her a pint and a packet of fags. How had she looked the night their father embraced her for the first time? Like a tart, a seductress, or daddy's little Lolita?

Mili's heart had hardened against her sister, and it wasn't only because of her behavior with her dad. Mardie had always criticized their mum, called her heartbreaking names because of her enslavement to sweets and her grotesque obesity. She harangued both her and her mother about being left out of their activities, yet screamed like a banshee and told them to go to Hell when they tried to explain why they felt alienated from her.

Oh, but now it was all different, wasn't it? She stood begging, clinging to the illusion that their brief reunion down here was something more than a forced truce. It was a hallucination that Mardie had conjured up in order to believe that things between her and Mili were different. The truth was that Mardie hadn't expended one single word to address the poisoned, bitter years of their childhood, let alone apologize for her conduct. They had no relationship.

Mili used her crutch and walked over to confront her twin. She looked her straight in the eye. Mardie stared back at her, face anxious and mouth shut, terrified of what her sister was about to say.

"I will try and accept," Mili said, "insofar as I am able, that what you did may not have been what you wanted to do." Then her eyes narrowed and her voice became severe. "But that does not expurgate my disgust for your despicable actions, nor does it make me feel sorry for you."

Tears flooded back into Mardie's eyes. Yet she refused to despair. Despite the cruelty of Mili's words, her sister had not closed the door on her. She watched her twin without speaking, clinging to her desperate hopes. Mili went on.

"In a few hours we will likely face the incarnation of the alternate Hugh Everett in this very spot. While Lucifer has not yet returned with God's verdict, I've decided that no matter what Jehovah decides, I am going to try to eliminate that murdering bastard, even if I have to do it myself." Mili stared at Mardie. Had she really just said that no matter what God ordered she was going to try to kill alternate Everett? Mili gave her no opportunity to respond. "Until this is over," she said in a tough, commanding voice, "and no matter how it ends, do whatever I tell you without a moment's hesitation. Do you understand?" Mardie nodded almost imperceptibly. Without another word Mili turned away and walked back toward Lucifer's home.

She felt a hand on her shoulder. She turned. It was Pfotenhauer.

"Give her the space she's asking for. She'll deal fairly with you when the time comes."

"I don't want her to deal fairly with me. I want her to forgive me."

Chapter Twenty-Three

Pfot nodded, took her arm, and led her back to the car. He helped her into the Volvo, then got in and started the engine. He glanced in the mirror at Mardie sitting quietly in the backseat, then drove off. He kept his eyes on the road, but his mind was stuck on Mardie's desperate conundrum, and how, in trying to comfort her, all he had done was given her false hope. Mardie was right in believing that the only way to get beyond the impasse between she and Mili was for her sister to forgive her. But he knew, having betrayed friends and colleagues to her for more than twenty years, that redemption was the one thing that Mili Wickett had never given to anyone. There was not and never would be any forgiveness for Mardie in the soul of Scotland Yard's most famous detective.

Chapter Twenty-Four

Pfotenhauer picked up Mardie at nine in the morning, only five hours after he'd taken her home. She came out of her house wearing a white blouse, navy slacks, and black flats. He could see that she was tired, and unhappy, but despite her woes she had still taken care to apply fresh makeup. Good on 'er, Pfot thought. Racing toward disaster, she was doing it looking like a lady.

Mardie greeted him kindly when he opened the car door for her, but that was all she said. Pfot closed the door and drove off. Neither he nor Mardie spoke as he made his way along the broken city roads to pick up the other passenger expecting him, Hugh Everett III. The big man was waiting on the sidewalk. He got in the front with Pfotenhauer. He noticed that Mardie was asleep in the backseat. Gosh, he'd had a great time with her last night. He had no idea how many Crown Royal Perfect Manhattans they'd drunk, and he didn't really recall a lot of specifics from their conversation, but he did recall quite clearly that she'd made him glow with happiness. How many women had ever done that to him before? It was easy to count to zero, even for a disgraced quantum physicist.

Mardie twilighted during the trip, being too physically and emotionally exhausted to fall into a deep sleep. It had been that way

Chapter Twenty-Four

all night as well, her mood shifting from sad, to angry, and back to sad. Why had she acted so desperate around Mili? It wasn't like her twin was going to remain down here, even if things did get patched up between them. The common sense thing would be to pursue a nice, even meaningful, relationship with Hugh rather than suffer endless anxieties over Mili's rejection or acceptance. He was surprisingly kind and gentle, and she liked that he seemed so cheerful. She knew he couldn't always be that way, but it pleased her to think that he acted that way because he was glad to be with her.

Even with such considerations, Mardie knew that she still needed Mili. She'd lived her entire life believing that she had been rejected by her. But these last few days Mili had been gracious, accepting, and seemingly happy to be in her company. That unexpected grace, that unexpected closeness, felt so real Mardie had allowed herself to believe that all the years of sadness and separation could be healed. Had Mili felt the same? What was in her heart before she got her hands on the police records? Suddenly the memory of her father's hard embrace and desperate thrusting crushed the air out of her. She saw his face, shrank back in fear and disgust, then gasped as his expression turned hideous, distorted with pain and horror as she plunged the knife into his neck.

Mardie cried out and woke up. Pfotenhauer looked back at her, as did Hugh. She closed her eyes rather than explain, but the same horrible images flooded back into her mind all over again. She opened her eyes and sat up. Both Pfot and Hugh tried to speak to her. She waved off their questions with her hand and stared out the car window. The dark and shadowy mountains on the horizon beckoned to her, *flee, child, flee.* She would have liked nothing better, but she knew there was no place to truly flee. Wherever she ran it would still be Hell, and like every other damned soul, she was stuck here forever. There were no in-and-out privileges. Except, of course, for the homicidal bastard who had found a way to crack Hell's cosmic door and trash the Devil's property with dead bodies.

Mardie shook her head, amused despite her turbulent feelings. In some pathetic way she owed that prick. Without his nefarious penetration of Hell, Mili would never have been brought down here to help, nor would she and Mardie have shared these last days that had been so special. Good had truly flowed out of evil. Such an occurrence had never happned to her before. Was it over forever? She had heard the reenactment people say that God didn't close a door without opening a window. Maybe for them. Not for her.

The slaughterhouse was busy when they arrived. Trucks were bringing in live cattle. Other trucks were carting out butchered carcasses. Pfotenhauer pulled the car into a visitor's parking place and went to sign in. Everett rolled down his window and lit up a cigarette. The outside air felt heavy, smelled like dust, and stank like death. Hugh took a deep drag on his cigarette and wondered how many cattle were being staged for processing, and how many would die if a nuke went off.

Pfotenhauer returned and they headed to the meat locker where the cadavers were stored. Everett walked inside and started yanking off the white plastic sheets covering the naked, semi-frozen bodies. He didn't seem bothered by the sight of the damaged corpses, not by the victim without a head, nor by the body laid out with its body parts detached. Hugh carefully scrutinized each of the cadavers. He examined injuries and inspected the results of the flaying, cutting, and burning they had endured. He turned and saw Mardie staring at him, as if to say, how can you do this?

Chapter Twenty-Four

"I barbecued a lot," he offered by way of explanation. Mardie just shook her head.

When she had first met Everett, he seemed devoid of normal feelings. But after drinking with him last night, Mili discovered that he had at least one great passion, to observe and understand everything he saw, even, apparently, dead people. Maybe that wasn't so strange given what Hugh had told her about his past, calculating casualties for Pentagon war games. A few years of that horseshit would give anyone a thick skin.

She watched Everett reach out a finger to touch a black patch of burned skin on one of the corpses.

"Don't!" Mardie yelped. "There's a box of gloves on that desk." She pointed at it behind them.

Everett saw the desk and walked back.

"Whoa," he exclaimed, reaching down and picking up the holiday picture. "One ugly batch of beasties, eh?" he said, and chortled loudly. He flashed the photograph of the demons at Mardie and laughed again. That from the incredible hulk, she thought uncharitably.

Everett grabbed a pair of latex gloves. He had trouble pulling them on. His fingers were perpetually swollen as a result of his unhealthy lifestyle. They had been bloated in his last life too, harbingers that he was going to drop dead of heart failure at age fifty-one. Now they were just ten obstacles preventing him from getting the latex gloves on. Everett managed, though he had to ask Mardie for help.

He explored the burned patch of flesh that he was interested in, examining it as minutely as a medieval monk eyeing the surface of a grain of wheat on which he was about to carve the Twenty-third Psalm. After that, Everett rapidly grew less circumspect, poking his fingers into the corpse's lacerations, burns, and punctures, as well as snooping inside its mouth, nose, ears, and anus. God Almighty, Mardie thought. Not much was private when you were alive, but apparently nothing was off-limits when you were dead. When he was finished, Everett shucked off the gloves and tossed them on the floor.

"Nothing," he grumbled, "although the deceased were relatively young, consistent with the age and appearance of the alternate described by the demons." He winked at Mardie. "Don't go falling in love with the slimmer, handsomer version of me when he shows up!"

Mardie laughed. Everett joined her, his eyes twinkling.

"We need to go now," Pfotenhauer said, and gestured toward the meat locker door. Everett opened it and walked out. Mardie bent down and picked up the gloves he had thrown on the floor. She dropped them into a trashcan by the desk and glanced again at the picture of the demon partiers. At least someone in this place was having fun. She followed Pfotenhauer and Everett to the car, only realizing when they were well on their way to Lucifer's house that the handgun and bullets she'd seen on the slaughterhouse desk the first time she'd been here were gone. Apparently the cattle being trucked into the rendering plant were kaput, just like Nils Bohr. And just like them, there wasn't a single thing he or anyone else could do about it.

It was the oddest queue Mardie had ever been in, waiting with a quantum physicist, two demons with machine guns, Lucifer, the Lord of Hell, an ex-mobster turned chauffeur, and Mili, her twin, who was poised to crack the greatest case of her career and very likely break her sister's heart at the same time. Mardie was sitting on a folding chair drinking black tea, keeping an eye on her twin who was sitting in her wheelchair on the far side of the porch. She'd already been waiting when

Chapter Twenty-Four

Mardie arrived and ignored her, focused on her iPad. Lucifer came out of the house wearing a night-robe, looking uncharacteristically tired. He bent over next to Mili and whispered in her ear. Then he straightened up and went back into the house.

Pfot sat down by Mardie. He told her that one of the security guards texted him saying that the Devil had only just returned from an all-night session with Jehovah. All night? What could those two have talked about? Actually, she didn't care what they talked about. It would be the same damn stuff they had been talking about since the beginning of time, God shaking His head over the likes of Nimrud, and Nebuchadnezzar, and Stalin, and Hitler, and Mao. The Devil, secretly gloating, listening to Jehovah complain, would then add his own two cents by sharing petty tales of sinful men, anecdotes about how this or that nobody on Earth had somehow managed to cheat his neighbor, sleep with his wife, or just drink him under the backyard picnic table.

When Satan did not reappear right away, the two security demons, supposedly vigilantly anticipating the appearance of the murderer, set their Da.Doom guns down and began morphing into famous personalities, each trying to guess the other's incarnations: Angelina Jolie in a red evening gown, Michelle Rodriguez in her Avatar flight suit, a bare-chested Vin Diesel flashing tattoos, Kelly Ripa in workout duds, Kourtney Kardashian in short shorts and high heels, Jimmy Kimmel—"

"Who the Hell are those people?" Everett complained loudly. He'd gone without alcohol since the night before and was signaling this deprivation with his belligerent mood. Mardie observed his conduct with disappointment. He was squandering the capital he had earned with his charm last night. "Show us somebody we know, "he demanded.

Immediately the 1950s were on parade. Glenn Ford appeared in a cowboy outfit, Jimmy Stewart stood tall in a cavalry officer's uniform. Betty White flaunted her youthful curves in a red-and-white polka dot bikini, and Brigitte Bardot flaunted hers *without* a bikini. George Reeves flexed his biceps in a Superman suit, and Hopalong Cassidy just sat on his horse and looked cool.

"Yes!" Everett cried. "Now do some politicians." Up popped Dwight Eisenhower in an army general's attire, Winston Churchill posed in black tails, a silk top hat, and a cigar, and Charles de Gaulle was outfitted like a French Foreign Legionnaire, complete with his signature pillbox cap and black leather bill. Everett clapped his hands and cried, "Bravo!"

The pair of demons reverted to their natural appearance faster than Mardie's eyes could follow when Lucifer walked back out of the house. He had changed into a royal-blue robe with a heavy gold chain around his neck hung with a medallion emblazoned with the face of Medusa. He was carrying a book, which he promptly began reading as soon as he sat down. After a few moments he smiled and his eyes twinkled with amusement. Then he laughed out loud and shook his head. Mardie squinted at the title on the spine. *Nothing to be Frightened Of.* She'd read that book, an enjoyable, somewhat tongue-in-cheek treatise by an English author named Julian Barnes. He had written in an erudite and entertaining style that there was very likely nothing to see, do, or worry about beyond the grave.

Mardie was sorry that she hadn't brought a book, too. Her iPhone screen was too small to comfortably read a downloaded novel or magazine. Maybe Mili would loan her an iSomething. It seemed absurd to think of broaching any subject given her earlier outburst, but Mardie realized that was exactly why she would dare

Chapter Twenty-Four

to ask. She had to know what her sister was thinking about her. She picked up her folding chair and set it down next to Mili's wheelchair. Mili didn't look at her. That should have been a telling clue for Mardie, but the heart does what the heart wants. No wonder so many hearts have been broken.

"I am sorry I disappointed you," Mardie said. Mili turned her head slowly, and stared at her twin. It was a look of sheer repugnance.

"Why not just apologize for your whole disappointing life?" Mili snapped.

Mardie was staggered by the viciousness of the attack.

"I beg your pardon?" she managed to ask.

"It's not *my* pardon that you need," Mili hissed. "Why don't you go find our mother for a start and apologize for seducing her husband?"

Mardie gasped as though Mili had robbed her of the power to even breathe. Gasping, she tried to defend herself.

"Mili, I was eleven years old," she cried. Every pair of eyes on the porch turned to the twins. "And *he* was the one who came and sat on my bed. He talked to me. He comforted me." Mili was listening, but her disdain was etched onto her face. Mardie began to sob. She didn't want to, but her sister's fury and her own terrible memories sapped her strength. "Night after night he came. He talked to me and he held me, until one night it went too far. I knew it was wrong, and I begged him not to, but he did, and I didn't try to stop him." Mardie put her face in her hands and began to weep.

Pfot stood up, wanting to comfort Mardie, but a glance from Lucifer sat him down again.

"And then, after years of saying yes," Mili said, "one night you decided to say no, and put a knife in Dad's heart."

Mardie nodded without speaking.

Mili's face went rigid. It was the mask of the judge, the executioner, and the undertaker. Her decision about Mardie had been made.

"I don't know how you escaped judgment for your crimes in life, but I'm glad you are damned for them now." She glared at her unprotesting twin, and poured every ounce of hatred she could muster into her last words. "I hope you rot in Hell forever."

And then it happened. With absolutely no sound at all, Hugh Everett III's alternate self appeared out of nowhere, a dozen feet away at the end of the porch. He was dressed in the same dark suit, white shirt, and black tie as before, and just like last time, he was pushing a wheelbarrow full of butchered body parts.

Lucifer jumped to his feet. His guards hoisted up their guns and aimed at the intruder. The man stopped and stared in surprise at the crowd on the other end of the porch. He lowered the wheelbarrow, then reached in his pants pocket for a handkerchief. He wiped the sweat from his face and pushed his black horn rim glasses back up the bridge of his nose, glancing at the faces watching him. Then he discovered the older version of himself scrutinizing his every move. He stared with amazement. Everett and Everett, *mano a mano*. Alternate Everett smiled, then began to laugh, the same huge laugh as Earthly Everett. He was delighted that his descent into torture and murder had ironically rewarded him with the appearance of another Hugh Everett III, demonstrating beyond any doubt that there were other worlds, with other Everetts.

Grimacing at his amused alternate, Earth's Hugh Everett III rose slowly from his chair. He was holding the gun he'd taken from the slaughterhouse. With a slow, unhurried motion, he aimed it at the smirking version of himself and fired. The murderer's expression turned to panic and he threw up his hands in an effort to protect himself. The bullet plowed into his chest. A wave of blood

Chapter Twenty-Four

raced across his white shirt. The injured man turned and staggered away. Everett ran after him, firing the pistol. The killer was hit again and again. He dropped to one knee, forced himself to rise, then lurched forward into nothingness and was gone.

"Two can play that game!" Everett cried, chasing the vanished man. He plunged into the place that had swallowed his double and disappeared. Now *he*, too, was gone, and right behind him was Mili.

"No, Mili, no!" Mardie screamed.

Her sister did not respond, shoving her wheelchair into the cosmic gateway that had already absorbed both Everetts. She disappeared.

Mardie turned to Lucifer, who stood stunned by what he had seen. She fell to her knees and held out her arms.

"She'll never be able to return!" she cried. "Please, please go after her!"

Lucifer looked at Mardie's face. He knew that Mili had rejected her, had acted with genuine hatred toward her, yet he could see without any doubt that Mardie still truly loved her sister. The Devil allowed himself to feel the wonder of that for one long moment, then smiled at Mardie and transformed into a fiery figure so brilliant she had to shield her eyes with her hands. With an astonishing leap, Lucifer plunged into the hidden folds of space that had swallowed the murderer, Everett, and Mili. In a single fleeting instant he, too, was gone.

Mardie wailed in despair. Pfotenhauer walked over, knelt down next to her, and put his arm around her shoulders. Mardie turned her face into his chest and wept, wept for the sister who had come back into her life only to spurn her, wept for the loss of the love and forgiveness she had had within her grasp and had now lost. After a while she allowed Pfotenhauer to help her to a chair. She continued to weep, overwhelmed by what had happened and desperately afraid of the future. Would Lucifer be able to save Mili? Would any of them find their way back? Everett had told her that there were endless alternate realities for every person, scattered across hundreds of billions of galaxies and thousands of trillions of stars. The magnitude of that struck Mardie like a slap in the face. She stopped crying and sat still, shocked into numbness. Wherever they had gone chasing the murderer, nobody was going to return. Not Lucifer, not Everett, not Mili. Not one of them. Not ever.

Chapter Twenty-Five

M ARDIE RETURNED TO LUCIFER'S HOUSE at ten o'clock every morning for a year. Pfotenhauer drove her each day and stayed in the car while she sat on the porch and waited for the Devil to bring Mili back. She cried herself to sleep for weeks after Mili's scathing last remarks to her, but Mardie rejected her sister's claim that their time together had no value. She and Mili had begun to reconcile after all their years apart. It was true that Mardie had hated her mother, and then her father, but she had never hated Mili. She'd *lost* Mili, and it was only in Hell, of all places, that she had discovered her again.

She often thought about her sister and tried to imagine what she was doing wherever she was. Was she staying with an alternate Mardie, or had she spurned her, too? She was even less sure what Lucifer might be doing. Had following Mili and the Everetts into the space portal gotten him in hot water with Jehovah? That Jehovah, or *The* Jehovah? And what about Hugh Everett? Had he managed to finish off his murderous alternate? She suspected that he had. Did that make him a hero or a wanted man where he had gone?

During the Devil's prolonged absence, a Council of Demons functioned in his place. Most of Hell's residents noticed that the quality of products and services declined, which was saying something. Virtually every damned soul longed for the good old days. Mardie agreed, though she'd been spared the privations others faced since the council had continued to honor Lucifer's contract with Mili. Heaven's provisions arrived without interference and she'd been allowed to keep Mili's big girl toys. She tried out hangman and liked it, especially when she was able to recruit real hangmen down here to play against. Her favorite was the Jewish Iraqi executioner who had pulled the lever on Saddam Hussein. Yes, he had confided in her, the dictator's head really had ripped off when he'd been hanged. Talk about insult to injury.

Mardie became a fixture at the Good News Club and a devoted fan of Biblical reenactments. It had a wonderful repertory, including *Delilah Tricks Samson*, where the evil temptress goes crazy trying to find out the secret of the big guy's strength, until smitten with desire, Samson reveals it's because of his constant devotion to God, *and* that he's never cut his hair. Oy vey. Then there was the story *Ruth Counsels Naomi*, where a nimble-witted older woman advises her younger friend to sleep at the feet of a man named Boaz, thereby winning him by demonstrating her desire to love and serve him. Pfotenhauer expressed a contrary opinion about what part of Boaz Ruth was supposed to cuddle. The romantic in Mardie didn't want to hear it, whether Pfot was right or not. The headlining show, *Moses in the Court of Pharaoh,* continued to play to sellout crowds, except for a brief hiatus when Moses had been swallowed by his anaconda and had to be cut out.

The biggest and best event for Mardie, though, was her new relationship with Bowles, the handsome bartender. She remembered Hugh Everett fondly, but Bowles was the man she wanted to be with. He was tender in all his dealings with her, and the two

Chapter Twenty-Five

of them often returned to her house after a show to perform a reenactment of their own. She introduced him to fondue. He especially liked cake balls dipped in melted chocolate. She told him how much Mili had loved them. He, in turn, introduced her to Moroccan Hold 'Em, which had nothing to do with food *or* cards.

Occasionally, sitting at the kitchen table and having tea by herself, Mardie tried to memorialize her sister in writing. She'd left the bedroom intact hoping for her return and had gone to considerable expense adding a second bedroom for herself rather than believe that Mili was never coming back. She'd even left the handicap ramp in the front of the house, just in case. But she found herself unable to *write* anything about her sister, perhaps because she did not know if her twin was alive, or dead, or something else altogether. Her worst fear, of course, was that both she and Lucifer had met some terrible fate in the alien place they'd gone, ending their existences forever. No, actually her worst fear was that she would never have the chance to ask Mili's forgiveness one more time. Even if her sister refused again, which Mardie thought highly likely given the grievous nature of her offense, she wanted the opportunity to ask.

And so it went for almost seven years, until one day there was a knock at Mardie's door. She looked through the peephole, and though no one had ever topped Barney's cameo appearance way back when, this visitor beat the purple dinosaur hands down. It was Lucifer. Mardie flung open the door and stared at him. He looked the same, only instead of a fancy robe he was dressed in khaki slacks, a violet Polo shirt, and cream-colored Top-Sider loafers.

"I am so sorry," he said softly, looking at her with incredible tenderness. "I only just got back."

"Where is Mili?" Mardie whispered, tears welling up in her eyes.

"May I come in?"

"Yes," Mardie murmured, and stepped back. "Of course, of course."

Satan entered the foyer and Mardie led him to the living room. "Sit anywhere," she told him.

He took a place on the big leather Chesterfield. "Will you take some tea?"

"Thank you, no. Please sit and I'll explain everything."

Mardie sat herself in one of the wingback chairs across the coffee table from the Devil. Seeing that Hell's archangel had indeed returned was thrilling, but his evasive manner upset her, causing all of her carefully repressed anxieties about Mili to skyrocket.

"First, and most important," Lucifer began, "Mili is fine."

"Oh, thank God!" Mardie moaned, and hugged her chest with her arms.

"When she and I dashed out of here, pursuing Hugh Everett's alternate, we entered a world that seemed exactly like Earth. However, unlike our planet, it had no tolerance for multiple DNA embodiments of the same pattern. In other words, there could be no duplicates. Everett was nowhere to be seen and then Mili was gone."

"Gone?" Mardie asked, not comprehending. "Gone somewhere else?"

"No. Gone away. Dematerialized."

"But you said Mili was all right!"

Lucifer held a hand up. "In a moment, please. I am sorry to make you wait, but I need to explain things in order."

Mardie sat back, a haunted look on her face.

"The one person who hadn't disappeared was the *alternate* Hugh Everett. It was his world and I found him lying on the ground, dying. He'd been shot in the chest and back. He looked

Chapter Twenty-Five

up at me, barely conscious. I knelt down and ripped pieces off his shirt trying to stanch the bleeding."

"You tried to help that bastard?"

"Do I look like Jesus?" Satan countered. "I was trying to prevent that asshole from dying before I had a chance to give him a piece of my mind."

Mardie held her tongue and waited for the Devil to tell the rest of his story.

"First, I made it clear to him that he was a dead man, and that there was nothing that he or anyone else could do about it. I let him know that his murder spree had cost me the talents and friendship of your sister, and the wisdom and companionship of *my* Hugh Everett. You'll have to forgive my childishness, Mardie, but I also told him that dumping the bodies at my house really pissed me off."

"Oh." Mardie imagined the dying killer staring into Satan's eyes and hearing this stuff. She hoped there was more.

"He began gasping for breaths. I could see that he was almost gone. I got on my knees and put my face right over his, explaining with great satisfaction that just before he died I was going to fold him into an alternate reality that already had a Hugh Everett III. Have a long last look when you arrive, I said, and then kiss it all goodbye. He looked at me with fish-on-the-bottom-of-the-boat eyes, but he didn't speak. I couldn't tell if he couldn't talk or wouldn't talk, but whatever the reason, he didn't say a word. I watched him for a few more seconds, remembering all the carnage he'd jettisoned at my house, and then I dragged him into a hole that folded him into a reality where he would be disembodied. Even at that I couldn't help thinking that he'd gotten off easy."

"And he was gone?" Mardie said. "Poof?"

Lucifer nodded his head. "Poof. I like that. Poof, indeed."

"And what about Mili?"

"I went right to Jehovah and told Him what had happened, including that Mili and Everett had been lost. Though He had authorized the elimination of the alternate Everett, He was surprised that it had cost Mili her life. He subjected me to an Old Testament–style rant about me failing yet again, but in the end He agreed to create a new immortal body for Mili, but with one condition. He told me that she had compromised her place in Heaven while in Hell, raging at you with hatred and then chasing after the alternate man intent on murdering him."

Mardie stared at Lucifer. "God wouldn't let her back into Heaven?"

The Devil shook his head. "He locked her out for good. The only way He would bring her back at all was as a Hellion."

"And?" Mardie urged.

"I told Jehovah I would take responsibility for Mili and asked Him to create her Hellion body with just enough variation in its DNA to allow her to co-exist with her alternate in dead Everett's alternate world until I could find the opening that would bring us back here."

Mardie sat staring at Satan. She was clearly not happy.

"You could travel to Heaven and talk to God, but you couldn't get Mili and yourself back in Hell?"

"I didn't say I couldn't, but I did have to find the right person to help me, and it took a while to do that."

"You're talking about *our* Hugh Everett III."

"Yes, our Hugh Everett, and by our, I mean it in the warmest, fondest way possible."

"Because you needed his ass to help you find the way back here."

Chapter Twenty-Five

"Not just because of that, but I won't deny that I did need the big guy's help. The alternate Everett had discovered a hole that entered Hell that no one else knew about, and that no one else could find. Not even Jehovah. I searched for it myself for seven years, begging God the whole time to recreate Hugh Everett III's Hellion body and bring the Many-Worlds genius back to life. He did, finally. Him and His seven-year thing. And, of course, it only took Hugh two days to locate the portal. I was thrilled, and so was he, and in that there was no longer any alternate on that world with DNA identical to his, he chose to stay. The last I heard he had tracked down his wife, reunited with his daughter, and joined his son's band. Apparently, he plays a mean baritone sax."

"Seven years," Mardie muttered, ignoring the Devil's words about Hugh Everett. She shook her head and muttered, "What a waste."

"Not necessarily," Lucifer told her and stood up. "Come with me."

Satan reached out and took Mardie's hand. He led her out the front door and waved to Pfotenhauer, who was standing at the curb next to the old white Volvo. Grinning wildly, he opened one of the back doors and out stepped Mili, or at least a woman who Mardie thought might be Mili. Her missing foot had been restored and she looked younger, thinner, and pretty once again. Some punishment, Mardie thought. Whatever God had done to Mili she'd willingly get in line for the same penalty herself. She shook her head and looked at Lucifer. "Did I fail to mention that I suggested certain alterations to Mili's Hellion body?" he asked.

Mardie looked at Mili's happy face and youthful figure, and then back at Satan. "Holy shit."

"I had a few suggestions for Everett's appearance, too. You should see him, young, robust, big bushy beard."

Mardie shook her head. "And Jehovah was all right with these *suggestions?*"

"Oh my no. Not at first anyway. I had to remind Him that both Mili and Everett had helped rid Creation of the folding man and told Him that authorizing a few bits of cosmetic work on their behalf would be an easy way to acknowledge their contributions." Lucifer went silent, watching Mardie. She returned his gaze, sensing that he was holding something back. Suddenly he chuckled and his eyes twinkled. "I also have Jehovah's permission to redo one more Hellion," he said, "as a thank you to someone without whose help this case would have probably never been solved." Mardie's eyes went wide. Lucifer smiled, kindly. "Yes, you. When and if you wish."

Before Mardie could respond Mili called from the car, waving and smiling. Out of the car stepped a little girl, blond and beautiful, wearing a white blouse and a pleated navy skirt, with white socks and black patent leather shoes.

Mardie's tears flowed freely as she ran down to the car. Tears running down her own cheeks, Mili reached out and folded Mardie in her arms. Lucifer picked up the little girl, and together they watched the twins hug, and cry, and hold each other. The sisters separated for a moment and gazed at each other. "I'm so sorry," they said in unison. They both laughed with surprise, then hugged again, weeping and sighing.

After a few moments, Lucifer whispered in the girl's ear. She nodded, then spoke in a clear, sweet voice, with a very proper English accent, "Hello, Auntie Mardie. We came to see you. May we come in?"

Chapter Twenty-Five

Mardie reached out her arms and took her. "Why, of course you may," she cooed, kissing her cheek. "What is your name, darling?"

"My name is Mardell Wickett," she said, and smiled grandly. "But I'd prefer it if you called me Mardie."

"Oh, honey," Mardie said, and hugged her close. "I am so glad you're here! We have so much to talk about."

"That we do," Mili said, speaking up.

Holding her little niece tight, Mardie slid her other arm around Mili's waist. "Lucifer told me you were staying. Did he really mean it?"

Mili nodded and smiled. "I'll be hanging around here, sis. Better get used to it."

Mardie shook her head, feeling lightheaded. "And this wonderful child is your daughter?"

Mili nodded, happily. "Mardie, show your auntie what you can do."

She asked to be put down, then shot up in flames like a tree on fire. Laughing, she waved her arms and twirled around.

Mardie looked at Lucifer. "Don't think we need a DNA check here."

"No, we don't," Lucifer said, beaming. He held up his hand and showed Mardie his gold wedding ring. "A wife, a different world, and then this little gem. Who knew?"

Mardie shook her head and smiled. Little Mardie stopped her spin and let herself flame out.

She ran back to her aunt and asked, "Is it true that my mom once ate a dozen chocolate-dipped cake balls at your house?" Her eyes were wide and excited.

"Actually, she ate two dozen, and it's still the record."

"Oh, may we have some now, Auntie, please, please?" little Mardie implored. Mardie looked at her sister, and Mili looked at her daughter.

"First we will have a proper meal, say meatloaf and mashed potatoes, with soup and a salad. Then, for a very special treat, we will all have one delicious cake ball dipped in chocolate."

"Only one?" Mardie asked, terribly disappointed. "Daddy?" she asked, instantly appealing the decision to her father.

"You heard your mother," he said gently but firmly. "Two cake balls."

Mili's eyebrows shot up, and Mardie grinned.

"What about three?" little Mardie responded, instantly upping the ante.

Lucifer held his hand out to his daughter, laughing, and led her into Mardie's house with Mili and Mardie following. "Two, not three," he told her. "Where do you think we are? Heaven?"

No, not Heaven, Mardie thought, pulling the door closed behind her. Even better. We're home.

The End

Acknowledgements

I WOULD LIKE TO THANK THE PEOPLE IN MY LIFE who in one way or another helped me write this book. Teacher, Verna Mae Walters; scholar and author, Dartmouth Professor James Heffernan; poets Robert Siegel and Richard Eberhart; everyone who read, commented, and encouraged me; my wife, Buff; my daughters, Michelle and Trace; my sons, Nik and Blake; my aunt, Lorraine Petrakis and her husband Peter Haggard; my friends, Callie and Sheridan Oakes, Shamus Owens, William and Karen Mitchell, and author and friend, Alan Rose, whose advice improved virtually every page in this novel; my special thanks to my two super readers, my mother-in-law, Bobette Jones, and my friend, Liliane Novak; and last, my heartfelt appreciation to creative logo artists Trace Jones and Andrea Juarez, world-class cover artist Vincent Chong, and the publisher who believed in me, Lionel A. Blanchard.